Seaside Ties

Nellie Brooks

Merpaper Press LLC

Copyright © 2023 Nellie Brooks.

This is a work of fiction. Names, characters, and places are products of the author's imagination. Any resemblance to actual persons, living or dead, events or locales is entirely coincidental. Any references to historical events, real people, or real places are used fictitiously.

All rights reserved. No part of this publication may be reproduced, distributed, or transmitted in any form or by any means, including photocopying, recording, or other electronic or mechanical methods, without the prior written permission of the publisher, except in the case of brief quotations embodied in critical reviews and certain other noncommercial uses permitted by copyright law. For permission requests, contact the publisher at MerpaperPressLLC@gmail.com.

Edited and proofread by *Karen Meeus Editing* and *Eagle Eye Proofreading*.

Published by Merpaper Press LLC.

Contents

Chapter 1	1
Chapter 2	9
Chapter 3	15
Chapter 4	26
Chapter 5	35
Chapter 6	41
Chapter 7	48
Chapter 8	56
Chapter 9	61
Chapter 10	68
Chapter 11	74
Chapter 12	79
Chapter 13	84
Chapter 14	94
Chapter 15	103
Chapter 16	112
Chapter 17	118
Chapter 18	125
Chapter 19	132
Chapter 20	138

Chapter 21	148
Chapter 22	154
Chapter 23	162
Chapter 24	172
Chapter 25	178
Chapter 26	185
Chapter 27	193
Beach Cove Home	198
Chapter One	199
Chapter Two	211
About the Author	218

Chapter 1

Summer was beautiful at the coast of Maine, and had it not been for the rain and the funeral, the arrival of June would have been a reason to celebrate in the small town of Beach Cove. The rugged cliff tops had dressed up in apple blossoms and hydrangea buds, the pretty front yards swayed green and lush, and sand and surf were finally warming. Tourists trickled into inns and motels, strolling along beaches and sometimes even braving a swim. Local businesses dusted their shelves and opened their doors to let in the fresh air. Generally, the world seemed ready to explode in a summery riot of heat and color.

But not on this particular day. A thick blanket of clouds muted the sunlight, and the soft tapping of rain blended with the sighs and rustling umbrellas of the mourners as they walked over wet pine needles and last year's maple leaves to gather around a fresh grave in the small cemetery behind the old white church.

Martin Sullivan had owned the town's candy store, and in his old age, been a sweet, kind person. His family and friends tossed their soil and their flowers in his honor, bowed their heads and wiped their tears, and when it was over, they hurried back to their cars to drive across the windswept cliff from Beach Cove to Bay Harbor.

Martin's granddaughter Mela had asked everyone to gather in the blue beach house on twelve Seasweet Lane, and so they did, loudly remembering their friend as they ate cake and sipped hot tea while quietly wondering when it would be their own turn.

Kitty, his other granddaughter, dried the last washed plate and put it into the kitchen cabinet. She was glad for the task. The steady stream of stories in the living room eroded her defenses, and all she wanted was to be alone so she could grieve on her own. She didn't care that Martin had been old and ready to go; she still needed him. Now there was nobody left who knew her from before. Nobody who knew both her parents, nobody who had witnessed her childhood. Never again would she have someone who shared her memories.

Sinking back into herself, Kitty stared out the kitchen window, seeing nothing but the dripping curtain of raindrops.

"Are you okay?" Kitty's half sister Mela stood in the door, an empty coffee carafe in one hand, a plate of leftover peach-swirl crumbs in the other. The scent of cream and baked fruit clung to her like a wholesome mantle.

Kitty herself only smelled of dishwasher liquid.

She sighed and held out her hand. "Yep. Here, I'll wash this."

"Forget the plate. You've done enough." Mela placed her things on the table, out of Kitty's reach. "Listen, Ellie and Gordy just left."

"Last ones?"

"Yes, they were the last ones. Guests, anyway. It's only family now."

"Oh. Okay." Kitty hadn't mingled for long. She only recently moved to Bay Harbor. It had been a difficult, stressful move that cost her both emotionally and financially. She couldn't stomach being social. Maybe that was the reason she still didn't belong.

"Sorry, Mela. The stories got to me."

"Aww." Mela marched over to where Kitty stood and pulled her into a hug. "No worries, my dear. Of course I understand. We all do."

Kitty wasn't a hugger by nature or custom, and the sisterly embrace made her eyes swim. "Um." She wiggled free and coughed a half-hearted apology. "Thank you."

Mela's friend Amelie entered the kitchen with a load of tea mugs. When she saw them, she pressed her lips together in commiseration. "Can I do anything for you? Would you like to sit down and eat something? Kitty? A hot cinnamon bun, maybe?"

"Oh. No, I couldn't eat another bite."

After she had sold her house in Seal Harbor at a loss, Kitty stayed with Mela for two months before finding a place of her own. It only took her two hours to understand that Amelie was considered family and that her love language was food. Kitty's eyes flicked to the table that practically teetered under the weight of hearty casseroles, sweet pies, and creamy comfort soups.

Mela had noticed the glance. "Sunny's out of freezer space. The kids will take some home, but you have to take some too or it'll spoil."

"As much as you can, Kitty," Amelie said warmly. "The kitchen in your apartment is barely set up. I know for a fact you don't own two pots to bang together."

"I do too. It's all still in boxes. It's fine." Kitty didn't want to lug home any of the heavy casseroles. She felt a little sick to the stomach.

Mela exchanged a long glance with her friend.

"Sorry," Kitty said again. "I'll take a bit of lasagna. The fridge is too small for the trays, and I don't want to leave it out on the counter to go bad."

"But can you really not stay here, at least tonight?" Mela put a hand on Kitty's arm. "Your room is just as you left it. The bed is freshly made and waiting for you. I even put a vase of fresh flowers on the nightstand."

Her younger sister had a steady stream of guests moving in and out of the house and was always prepared with a spare bed and a warm dinner for anyone in need. "Thanks, but I think I'll go home," Kitty declared, pulling herself together so she wouldn't attract any more offers of food and shelter. "My apartment is just around the corner."

"I don't like to think of you alone. Not tonight."

"Listen, I'm fine. Martin was in his nineties, and he died in his sleep, the way we all hope to go. I miss him, but I can handle it."

Amelie and Mela stood in front of her with identical frowns, studying her.

A smile—the first in days—tugged on Kitty's lips. "You two really are like the little sisters I never had."

Amelie smiled back, but Mela, still dissatisfied, pursed her lips. "Call me if you want to talk," she ordered. "Come over anytime, even if it's just to watch TV and eat ice cream together. You still have the key, don't you?"

Kitty had never used the key since the door was always open. She couldn't even remember where it was. Somewhere in the new apartment. "I meant to give it back," she said guiltily.

Mela shook her head. "Keep it. We never lock the house anyway, but just in case."

Kitty remembered now—the key was in the green bowl in the bathroom. She'd return it tomorrow. "You probably should lock the house. There were lots of break-ins in Seal Harbor. My neighbor's home was robbed while she was visiting her cousin over a long weekend. She lost her great-grandpa's painting, and it broke her heart. She's been searching thrift stores for years hoping to get it back."

"I'm not surprised. Seal Harbor is full of wealthy people," Amelie chimed in. "I'd go there too if I were a robber. But Bay Harbor is an old fishing village. I don't think there's much danger of break-ins. All they would find are unpaid bills and threadbare furniture. It's not worth the gas in the tank to come out here."

Amelie had lived all her life in Bay Harbor. Kitty, coming in with fresh eyes, thought the town did better than that—largely thanks to Mela's and Amelie's efforts.

"Yeah? What about your Charlie? He's not a poor lobster fisher." Kitty walked to the chair by the door and dug out her red anorak from the remaining rain jackets and coats. She missed bustling, artsy Seal Harbor even if she'd been priced out of town. And Charlie Townson, Amelie's partner, was clearly as wealthy as any of the millionaires that had taken over Seal Harbor after a well-known talk show host bought a house there.

"I guess he does lock the door," Amelie admitted sheepishly. "But only because he lived in Sydney for so many years."

"Sure." Mela grinned. "Not because he keeps showering you with diamonds and pearls and you keep letting them lie around."

"He doesn't shower me." Amelie grasped the new pendant glistening at her throat.

"If he doesn't, it's only because you won't let him. Let him! He obviously wants to." Kitty was glad the focus had shifted away from her. She slipped her arms into the sleeves that were still damp. Then she fished her phone from her pocket and glanced at the screen. The battery had died. Now there was nobody left to call other than Mela, so it didn't matter. She slipped it back before Mela could see the black screen and wonder whether her older sister wasn't able to pay her phone bill. "I think I'll leave now," Kitty said.

"Can't I at least drive you?" Mela dropped her arms in defeat.

Kitty shook her hair, the short brown curls falling into her face. "Thanks, Mela. I like to walk. Let's talk tomorrow afternoon. I want to know what happens at the farmers market."

Mela had bought out Kitty's stand at the farmers market, where she now sold honey and wax candles, pollen to sprinkle over breakfast cereal and healing propolis. Kitty used to sell her hats there, but her profits had taken a nose-dive that turned into a free-fall during the house sale and the move. The stress crushed her creativity and joy, and she had neglected her business until the checks coming in the mail were not even enough to buy materials.

Kitty kept that to herself too. Her younger sister was already treating her like a charity case.

"Wait, I'll find a bag for your lasagna." Amelie rushed off, but Mela hooked her arm under Kitty's as they walked to the door. "I hate thinking of you being alone," Mela protested as Kitty pulled up the anorak hood and stepped into the evening gloom. "Promise you'll come over the second you feel lonely."

A raindrop splashed off her hood's visor and into Kitty's eye. She blinked the water away. "You really are such a little sister," she said and gently bopped Mela's shoulder. "Stop bugging me. I'm fine."

"I know you are. That's not the problem." To Kitty's surprise, Mela leaned in and kissed her on the cheek.

Kitty flushed. They'd only met in their fifties when they found out they shared a father. With a difficult mother and a dad who chose a different wife and kid, Kitty didn't exactly consider herself a family person. More of a cheerful loner. At least cheerful when her grandfather, the last constant in her life, had still been alive.

Mela, on the other hand, seemed comfortable accepting Kitty as family.

"Hey, you did an unbelievable job today," Kitty said. "Martin would be so proud of you. And so grateful. You only knew him for a few months, but you made sure his friends had a place to come together and...well. You know."

Tears rose as sudden as a spring flood. Kitty turned away, letting the rain hide them.

"I'm grateful I met him. But you knew him better. Your loss goes deeper."

"See you soon, then." Kitty didn't look back even when Amelie came around the corner with the bagged lasagna. One more kind word, and she'd lose it.

She walked down Seasweet Lane, glancing up briefly when she passed number ten. Mela's daughter Sisley lived there. Sisley was engaged to Amelie's son, Bennett, and their wedding was scheduled for the end of the month. It would be a church wedding with a beach party afterward. Martin had ordered a new suit so he could dance with his great-granddaughter in style. Now he wore the suit in his coffin.

Kitty wiped the rain out of her eyes. The next house was lit up too. Morris, Mela's son, owned it. He was a pianist and lived together with his girlfriend, Johanna. Johanna used to be Mela's personal assistant, back when Mela was married to a New Hampshire senator. The windows in the next house also shone bright and inviting into the darkening afternoon. This one belonged to Kimmie, Mela's eldest daughter, who lived there with her ex-husband, Travis. After a tumultuous divorce for all the wrong reasons, the two had found each other again. When Kitty glanced up, she saw Travis's daughter Pippa looking out the upstairs window. Pippa waved and started singing a nursery rhyme at the top of her voice. It was so loud Kitty could hear it through the glass.

Kitty blew the little girl a kiss and hurried on.

Mela had used her time well. She built herself a rich and colorful life full of friends and family by the sea.

Unlike herself. Kitty turned around a soggy boxwood hedge as high as her head, accidentally brushing against it. She was rewarded with a cold shower of droplets. She shook it off. Another turn, and she was on Main Street. Shoulders hunched, she quickly strode along the empty sidewalk.

Martin had gotten dizzy the day the weather turned. With every hour, he became sleepier and quieter until he went to bed one stormy evening the previous week and never woke up again.

Dirty water splashed up Kitty's legs and into the cheap black pumps she'd bought for the funeral. Suddenly, she was furious. Why did she have to step into the stupid puddle? It'd been there for a week. Why couldn't she remember? Why hadn't she paid attention? And why were the sidewalks in Bay Harbor so crooked that there were puddles everywhere? That would never happen in Seal Harbor.

Steaming, Kitty bit her lip until she reached the house where she rented the upstairs apartment. Downstairs lived a kid in his twenties who talked too much about the girlfriend who'd left him.

Usually, Kitty didn't mind listening. But not now. She was cold, sad, and ready to scream her frustration out at the world. Her life was mostly over, and she had nothing to show for it. She needed to be alone. She needed a hot bath, a large glass of wine, and then she desperately needed to curl up in bed and cry her eyes out.

Kitty climbed the stairs as quickly and quietly as she could, carefully avoiding all the creaky boards. It wasn't until she ducked under the slanted gable of her apartment and locked the door behind her that she remembered she no longer had a bathtub. Only a shower. And no wine either—she'd forgotten again to go to the grocery store.

Shrugging off her damp anorak and dropping it on the floor, she went past the stacks of still-unopened moving boxes to the bedroom. She dropped face down on the bed as if she were fifteen, not fifty-five, kicked off the ruined pumps, and pulled the comforter over herself even though she was as wet and smelly as an old dog.

Slowly, her body warmed, unfreezing the first tears.

She did not try to stop them.

Tomorrow, she would pull herself together. She needed to do something about her business. Her sister had reinvented herself. Maybe Kitty could do the same. Start over.

New family, new business, new home.

But not tonight. Tonight, she needed to say goodbye to the past.

Chapter 2

"I can't believe you came." Valerie's mouth dropped as if it was trying to visit her chin.

"I did." Mela shoved the tarp cover sagging over her honey stand. "Watch out there." Last night's rainwater splashed to the ground, and her visitor squeaked. "That was more water than I thought!"

Valerie Sanders considered herself the first lady of the Bay Harbor farmers market. The chair of committees, the string holder. Each market day, she made sure to mention it in one form or another lest anyone should forget.

After the previous day's funeral and the difficult week leading up to it, Mela was in no mood to pretend she enjoyed the woman's visit. Maybe the market was the best in the area, and maybe Valerie had helped build it up. But the honey stand belonged to Mela.

"You got my sneakers dirty!" Valerie peered at her white brand-name boat shoes.

Mela sighed. "I'm sorry, Valerie. Can I help you with anything?"

"I was just... I only wanted..." Valerie huffed and tugged on the collar of her polo shirt as if her words had hidden below it and she meant to tumble them out.

A tourist was approaching the stand with a smile. With one glance, Mela could tell he was a beekeeper, moving in for a chat. She wanted to talk about beekeeping too, and she wanted to give him some honey. For free, just because he was smiling.

"I'm too busy to go home and change." Valerie glared at Mela like a cheerleader in a mean-girls movie.

"It's not that bad. Come on now." Mela shook her head at the shoes. Mostly, the bright white canvas was perfectly dry.

"You could have paid attention!"

Mela raised her eyebrows and closed her eyes before she opened them again. "It's a marketplace. There are cobblestones and crud. It's muddy because it has rained for a week straight. So why"—Mela rested her hands on the counter and leaned forward—"why, Valerie, are you wearing white canvas shoes? You know they can't stay pristine."

Valerie stared, and the beekeeper tourist who'd caught the last words frowned nervously. Mela grabbed a pot of honey with a yellow ribbon on it and thrust it at him. "On the house. Enjoy. Come again soon."

"Uh. Thanks." The man shrugged and sidestepped to the neighboring walnut-and-olive bread stand, tucking the honey into his tote bag.

Mela exhaled before she turned back. She never talked to Valerie like this. She never talked like this to anyone. But she was fresh out of patience. "Besides, if you have so much to do, why are you not doing it?"

Valerie's lips quivered once, and then she suddenly pulled them back up where they belonged and gave a breathy, girlish laugh. "I know, right?"

Mela unwound a kitchen towel from her apron band and wiped the dust off a couple of jars before she trusted herself to talk again. "Well, is there anything I can do for you?"

"Actually, since you ask..." Valerie glanced over her shoulder. There was nobody there. The rain was finally over, but most tourists had already made plans for the restaurants and museums in the bigger towns. "I do feel a little...well, not exactly overwhelmed, but maybe I took on more than I should. I thought I'd give someone else a chance at the fun jobs. Mela?"

"Yes?"

"How would you like to run the Bay Harbor pie contest?"

Mela tucked the towel back. "There's a pie contest?"

For a moment, Valerie looked pained. Then she rallied. "Yes there is. It's not affiliated with the market because it has gotten too big—and sometimes, it rains and we can't fit all the cakes under the awning. Plus, the market visitors get annoyed when the winning cakes sell out before they get a turn at buying their slices. Plus…" She leaned forward confidentially. "There have been unpleasant scenes. By the losing bakers."

"Oh no." Mela couldn't imagine what could happen. She knew most of the women in Bay Harbor. There was not a single woman who wouldn't lose with grace.

"Yes." Valerie nodded a confirmation. "So now, part of the responsibility has become renting a proper space." She straightened again and cleared her throat majestically. "Well, what do you say?"

Mela shrugged. It was an offer of peace from Valerie, strangely triggered by Mela losing her patience. If Mela had been all pretty please and thank you as usual with the market organizer, Valerie would never have made the offer. But Mela had enough on her plate. She didn't need another task. "Well, I just organized the funeral for my grandfather. My daughter's wedding is coming up. And you know my sister moved into town. I want to spend time with her. Also, the motel is booked out, and we're figuring all that out. I don't think I should take on anything more either, Valerie. I'm sorry."

Valerie blinked rapidly. "I thought you'd be excited about the opportunity."

"Maybe Sunny would like to do it."

"Your aunt? Wouldn't it be too much for her?"

Very little was too much for Sunny these days. Instead of slowing her down, every passing birthday seemed to give her more energy. "She'd be great if you could talk her into it. She's put it into her head to help the kids set up their houses. They're not going to thank you for stopping their auntie from spoiling them, but they're perfectly able to take care of themselves."

"I've never had to talk anybody into it," Valerie huffed. "It's an honor to chair the pie committee."

"It is work is what it is," Mela said dryly. "But if you like, I can ask her."

Valerie's throat moved as if she swallowed several choice words. "Fine," she finally relented. "If you would."

"I will. And Valerie..." Mela didn't know why she said what she said next. "Have you met Amelie Cobb? She's a therapist. She's great if you ever need to talk with someone about..." She caught her breath. It wasn't really her place or way to tell people things like this—even if she thought them. But something about Valerie's sudden change in demeanor tugged on Mela.

The thin eyebrows rose. "About?"

"Being overwhelmed," Mela finished after a moment of hesitation. "You don't usually worry about a spot of water on your shoes, do you? You're doing such a wonderful job with this market—there's no way you waste time worrying about that."

Mela bit her lip. She'd never been this familiar with Valerie. She'd never told her when she annoyed her. She also had never told Valerie she was doing a wonderful job. But if Valerie thought it was okay to make a fuss over her shoes, maybe they'd reached a new level of...something. Something that could turn out either way.

It was as if a mask slipped off the woman's face. Her eyes widened, her lips softened, but this time, there was none of that breathy laughter that sounded as if she needed to pacify an angry mother.

"Well, maybe," Valerie murmured. "I do have so much to do."

"It's okay to say no," Mela offered. "Amelie teaches women how to do it all the time. We're too old to be stressed, aren't we?" She smiled.

Valerie's eyes opened even wider. "Maybe," she said finally. "Yes, maybe. I..." She smiled back tentatively. "I'd like to visit my son. Georg. He's a doctor in the Bahamas."

"I'd go." Mela picked up a jar of honey and held it out. Valerie wasn't the only one who knew how to extend a peace offering. "Would you do me a favor and try this sometime? I put the bees in the field behind my house. The honey tastes of lavender and wood smoke. At least I think so. But I'd like to have your opinion before I put it in the description."

Valerie's fingers curled around the gift. "Do you have Amelie's number on you, by chance? I only know her from seeing her around."

"I do." Mela knew her friend's number as well as her own. She scribbled it on an empty jar label and peeled it off the paper backing.

Valerie tucked it into the pocket of her slacks. "Let me know what your aunt thinks about the pie contest."

"I will."

Valerie turned to go. "Mind you, I'd still have to check if it works even if she's interested."

"Okay."

"Okay." Valerie's lips formed the words before she said them. As if she needed to try them out first. "Thank you, Mela. For..." Valerie waved her pointer finger between them. "And also the smokey lavender honey. I'll let you know how I like it. See you around."

"See you, Valerie." Mela watched her walk away, then shifted some jars to fill the gaps and give herself time to recover from the exchange.

It was different now between her and Valerie. Better, for sure. Closer, and more of a back-and-forth than before. Each woman had allowed a look behind the facade. It exposed what was inside, for better or worse.

Better, in this case. The market manager was more human. They'd exchanged opinions and gifts. Almost like friends.

Mela put the last jar in place.

If she could crack the friendship code with Valerie, why couldn't she crack it with her own sister? Kitty had such a friendly, warm personality. The stress of the last months, topped off with the loss of her beloved grandfather, had shut her down. All her cracks had been mortared shut, and when they broke open by accident, Kitty was angry or embarrassed because she didn't want to share her real self. Not with Mela nor with her family.

It didn't feel personal. It felt like Kitty had lost herself. Her former life was over. Reeling from the loss, Kitty couldn't accept the new one.

Mela frowned. At this age, she wouldn't like to be in Kitty's situation either.

Offers of living together, of joining their family the way Sunny had done, seemed roundly rejected by her sister. She was too proud or too independent—or maybe she just didn't like Mela very much.

Mela felt the air leave her lungs as she deflated. She liked Kitty. She liked her a lot, and she was so ready to have a sister. What could she possibly do to help Kitty feel more comfortable? What could she offer to make her sister feel she was safe?

What was it her sister needed?

Chapter 3

"All right." Sisley let her gaze travel around her living room. It was crowded with women and purses, cakes and coffee cups and opinions. "This is getting out of hand."

Amelie set her cup back on the table and folded her hands like a patient parent explaining to their toddler one more time how things worked. "Bennett is my only child," she said. "I never married myself, and I only get this wedding. I've dreamed of it. Literally." She cleared her throat, half-embarrassed. "I'm sorry to put all my little-girl dreams on you, sweetheart. But I always pictured his bride wearing an Audrey-Hepburn dress on his big day. It's such a delicate neckline, and you of all people have the swan's neck to pull it off, Sisley. Just look at it—fine as a cobweb." She lifted the snowy-white fabric from her lap and held it out. "Here. Touch the lace."

"I already did. Several times." Sisley smiled to soften her exasperation. "Mom?"

"I don't have a horse in the running other than thinking you should wear something you like. I'll buy you something new if you want," Mom said cheerfully. "Sorry, Amelie. You can always marry Charlie and wear lace. I know he would be over the moon."

Amelie threw her a dark glance but didn't reply.

"I don't want to spend more money." After wasting her time on a disastrous relationship and then asking for a loan from her parents to start a business venture with her brother Morris, Sisley owned less than the clothes on her back. She was deeply conscious of it and determined not to be wasteful.

"What about your old wedding dress, Mela?" Sunny leaned forward to see her niece around the other women. "I haven't heard about that one yet. Maybe your daughter would prefer to wear that?"

Mela waved the question away. "Mine was super scratchy. I was clenching my teeth so hard, trying not to squirm like a landed fish; I barely even remember anything else about the ceremony. Besides, his mother picked it out. I left it in Robert's attic somewhere."

"You're only so relaxed because you'll also get Kimmie's and Johanna's weddings," Amelie complained and pointed an accusing finger at Kimmie, who looked surprised. Johanna quickly stifled a chuckle.

Amelie turned back to Sisley with pleading eyes. "I know you want to wear your grandmother Julie's white silk dress, Sisley. But the top is so '70s. To be honest, it's not even a wedding dress. The sleeves are puffy. Who wears puffy sleeves anymore? You'll look like someone from *Little House on the Prairie* when you could be so graceful."

"Sisley loves the skirt, though," Kimmie chipped in. "By the way, about your earlier comment there—I'd never wear Mom's dress. Do I seem like I'd want a scratchy dress? Or a train?" She shook her raven pixie cut. It looked even more spikey than usual, making her head resemble a grumpy hedgehog.

"A bit of a train wouldn't hurt you," Sunny murmured from the couch. She was slumped back comfortably. Her hands were resting on her belly, and the only sign of her interest showed in the way her thumbs rapidly twiddled around each other. "You're not going to march down the aisle like a biker chick. I won't allow it."

Kimmie narrowed her eyes. "A biker chick? You think I look like a biker chick?"

"Always with the black hair! You should stop dying it and let it grow out. It wants to be pretty." Sunny glared at her grandniece. Her many attempts at persuading Kimmie to change her style to beachy chic had been unsuccessful.

"It's urban. Uh, city-edgy," Mom tried to mediate, but Kimmie only groaned. "Besides...you're not getting married again—or are you, Kimmie?"

Kimmie looked around herself as though searching for the quickest exit route. "Why are we talking about me? This is about Sisley's dress."

"And this morning," Sisley broke in loudly because Johanna was laughing and things were well on their way to getting off track. "This morning, guess what arrived?"

"What?" Mom smiled fondly at her. "A wedding gift from Bennett? What is it? A watch? Watches are traditional, aren't they? Or was that something else?"

"A watch? Mom, we all have cell phones; nobody uses watches anymore. No. It was another dress!" Sisley dropped her arms. She'd not meant to reveal it in case she hated the new dress—she already had to decide between Julie's and Amelie's. But she didn't love the ridiculously puffy sleeves of the one or the vast swaths of lace in the skirt of the other. It reminded her of a tablecloth.

Since she was getting nowhere, she might as well throw it all out there.

"Aww honey, another dress. Who is it from?" Mom sat up expectantly.

"Dad."

"Dad sent you a dress?" Mom's eyebrows rose. "Did he find my old one in the attic? That would be a surprise. I can't imagine he went looking for it."

"Well, where is it?" Sunny's thumbs reversed direction. "Can I see it?"

"Sure. Kimmie, help me?" Sisley went into the guest bathroom, hearing her sister get up and follow.

The room was small, but there was enough space to change comfortably. The room reflected the light from the open window, and the salty air from the beach mixed with the marzipan scent of the almond soap on the sink.

Sisley swiped back the shower curtain, revealing the gigantic opaque dress bag she'd hidden there. "This is it."

"There's an entire dead person in there!" Kimmie laughed.

Sisley raised an eyebrow. "If it wasn't from Dad, I might be worried. Well, really, it's from Grandmother." Dad's parents had tons of money and extraordinarily little taste.

Kimmie took her hand. "Just let Mom buy you a new dress. She obviously wants to. You don't have to make do."

"I can't ask her to spend more when I have all these choices. There are things I like about both Julie's and Amelie's."

"Don't be stupid," Kimmie said with sisterly unconcern and let go to push the curtain back further. "You gotta love the entire thing. Here, grab this."

Together, they unhooked the dress bag from the shower rod and lowered it to the ground.

"Mucho pounds. Are you sure there's a dress in there?" Kimmie pretended to buckle under the weight. "Could be plated armor. Maybe it's meant for Bennett."

"No, it's a wedding dress. I peeked."

"Why is it so heavy, then?" Kimmie asked and sat on the closed toilet seat.

"It's encrusted. Like a dragon's belly."

"Encrusted with what? Treasure?"

"Bling," Sisley answered and unzipped the bag. The dress spilled from the crackling plastic like a glittering avalanche.

"Whoa. Careful it doesn't knock you out." Kimmie's lips twitched. "Oh. It smells of perfume." She sniffed the air.

"It's Grandma's old dress. I'm scared the bling is real. I haven't been able to eat anything since it arrived."

"Me neither. Did it come in an armored truck?"

"No, just the normal delivery service." Sisley tilted her head. "What do you mean, 'me neither'? Did Travis not make you breakfast in bed?"

Kimmie pursed her lips as if she regretted telling Sisley her partner spoiled her. "If they were real jewels on the dress, Dad wouldn't send it in the mail. Was there a note?"

"Yes." Sisley slipped off her morning robe and wrestled the fabric to find the opening. "But you know Dad. He only wrote it was Grandma's and she'd like me to wear it so she can remember the good old times. Though he didn't say it like that."

"Oh well." Kimmie laughed as she tugged the dress up. "If Grandmother really cared that much, she'd be standing here instead of me, staring at you without blinking until she gets what she wants. Hey, arm in here. Now... no, that goes there. Okay. Um. Let's not worry about doing up the one hundred thousand buttons."

There was the sound of a zipper closing, but Sisley couldn't feel the waist cinch in. Grandmother was a lot bigger than her. She had to hold up the dress so it wouldn't drop down to her ankles. The rhinestones and pearls pressed cold against the bare skin of her arms.

Kimmie squeezed past so she could see the front. She tilted her head critically. "Oh well. Does it feel good?"

"No." Sisley glared at her sister. "Is it closed? Or are you messing with me?"

Kimmie swallowed a smile. "Closed all the way. The buttons are only for decoration."

"What do you think?" Sisley turned in front of the mirror. "I feel like one of those beach snails that make themselves shells of random bits and pieces they glue together."

Kimmie giggled and hoisted the folded train into her arms. "Let's go show them."

Clutching the bust, Sisley waded back into the living room. Johanna was standing by the fireplace, whistling a little tune and tapping her fingers on the mantel. Mom, Sunny, and Amelie were talking about Valerie, the woman who ran the farmers market, but everyone looked up when she entered.

Kimmie dropped the train, letting it smack to the ground like a rolled rug. "Ta-da. Grandma's wedding dress."

"Aha." Mom nodded. "Sure. She picked my gown too. Hey—why didn't she offer her gown to me?"

Amelie patted her hand. "Never mind," she said. "That's obviously too much taffeta, Sisley. Wear mine instead."

"Turn around," Johanna ordered. "Let's see what we have in the back. Oh, wow. Ha-ha!"

"I don't know what you all want," Sunny declared. "I think it's great. Like Lady Di's dress with glitter. If I could have afforded a real wedding dress back then, that's exactly what I would have worn." The doorbell rang, and she narrowed her eyes. "It'd better not be Bennett! He can't see the dress before the wedding." She strode to the door.

"It's Kitty," Sisley said distractedly. "She texted me she would be late because the register at the Sandville supermarket broke and they had to wait for the computer to restart."

"Hello!" Kitty called. Her shoes hit the braided rug in the entrance hall with two soft thuds. "Sorry I'm late."

"Come in, Kitty. Glad you could make it," Sisley called back. She felt silly calling her Aunt Kitty, just like she didn't say Grandma Julie. That side of her family was more unconventional.

Mom looked up, a tiny frown pulling her eyebrows together. "Hi, Kitty. You could've come to Bay Port yesterday with Sunny and me. The Sandville supermarket is on the fritz since they started the construction in the back."

"I only needed a couple of little things." Kitty followed Sunny into the living room, and they sat. Kitty was wearing jeans and a cashmere sweater that looked cozy and threadbare with age and washings.

Sisley hoisted the dress higher.

"That's some wedding dress," Kitty noted. The laugh lines beside her blueberry eyes deepened.

Sisley smiled back. "Isn't it? If Bennett ditches me, the kids and I can live off the bling for twenty years before we have to worry."

"Bennett's not going to ditch anyone, least of all you," Amelie remarked dryly. "By the way, does he have an opinion about the dress? Did you two talk about what he wants?"

"I asked, and he said he doesn't care and just wants to elope." Sisley sighed. "But I'm to keep it a secret."

"Oh, he cares." Johanna smiled.

"Don't elope," Mom said mechanically.

Kimmie lifted the train. "Good golly, that's long."

"Yeah, I don't know about that train," Sisley said doubtfully.

Mom slapped the arm of the sofa and stood to inspect the dress.

"That's a chapel train. Kimmie, pull it over there." Amelie stood to tug on the stiff taffeta. Yard after yard unfolded, filling the space between the wall and the fireplace. "How is that supposed to work on a beach? You'll rake up all the seaweed."

"The brooch is gorgeous." Johanna squinted to see better. "I bet those are diamonds."

"There's a brooch?" Sisley squinted too. "Oh. I think that's attached. Part of the design."

With a huff of exhaustion, Kimmie lowered the dress. "The dress is too big, Sis. You'll drown in the fabric."

"Also in the sea if it gets wet," Johanna noted. "It'll drag you right down."

"Geez, Jo. With the tact and all," Kimmie muttered. Their grandparents, Julie and Finn, had drowned in the sea—though not wearing wedding dresses.

"Sorry," Johanna said sheepishly. "Sorry, Mela."

Mom wasn't paying attention. "We need to see the other dresses on you, Sisley," she decided. "Ideally in rapid succession. Go ahead and put them on."

An involuntary moan rose in Sisley's throat, but she swallowed before it escaped. That was why they were gathered, after all. The real problem was that she didn't love any of the dresses. Should she just close her eyes and pick one?

"Come on, Sis. I'll help you." Kimmie dragged the dress off toward the guest loo, pulling Sisley along. "Let's get this over with. You do want a dress, don't you?"

Sisley nodded and stuffed herself back into the bathroom. "You didn't wear one," she noted.

"I did too." Kimmie had picked something off the rack at a boutique in Soho for her civil ceremony with Travis. "You're welcome to my blue number, but I have to warn you. It didn't bring me any luck." She locked the door behind them.

"The skirt was so short." Sisley sank onto the closed toilet. "Maybe I'll wear jeans and a sweater. I don't like any one dress very much, and I don't want to offend anyone."

"It's your wedding. Don't worry about Grandmother and Amelie. In the end, they want you and Bennett to be happy. Let's just put on the other two dresses one more time, and then you decide. I'll go get them."

The next dress Sisley tried was Julie's; sewn from floaty white silk, it must've been her very best. When she went into the living room to show it, Sisley pictured herself walking on the beach while the breeze fanned the silk behind her.

"But it's not even a wedding dress," Amelie noted dejectedly. "Do you like the sleeves?"

"Not particularly," Sisley admitted. "I love the skirt. But the lace sleeves of your dress are much nicer."

"But Amelie's dress is a bit…" Mela cleared her throat and continued in a whisper. "It's a bit lacey, isn't it? Too much lace?"

Amelie's eyes widened. "I love lace! And so does Bennett!"

"Does he really?" Sisley asked. Her fiancé had never seen the dress his mother bought. "I mean, I do. But does he?"

"I think so." Amelie nodded. "He said something once. It's not like we talk very much about fabrics."

"Hmm." Sisley did like the delicate top. But the skirt still looked like a stiff, old-fashioned tablecloth…

Kitty picked up the dress. "Maybe…"

"What?" All eyes in the room turned to her. Kitty hadn't contributed yet.

"You should take what you like best from each gown. Julie's skirt and, um, Amelie, how about the top of yours?"

"Do you think that would work?"

"Oh," Amelie said. "Cut it? Oh, I don't know."

Sisley smiled. "I could use the brooch bling thing and some of"—she wiggled a slim gem-encrusted sash-looking band running down the side—"whatever this is, and turn the two into a belt."

"I can see it!" Johanna beamed. "I think it's a great idea!"

"So you would have Julie's silk skirt, Granny's bling belt, and Amelie's lace top," Mom summarized. "You know what? I think it could work too. I really do."

"Hmm," Amelie murmured. "Yes. The top is important."

"Exactly." Sunny patted Amelie's hand.

"Something old, something new, something blue," Kimmie said. "Blue for good luck."

"There's nothing blue," Johanna noted. "What's blue?"

"My dress," Kimmie said, satisfied. "You can cut a little square from it and sew it inside your sleeve or something. You're not allowed to turn it into a garter, though."

"I don't want a garter. But I'll make a heart from it." Sisley blew her sister an exaggerated kiss, and Kimmie, just as dramatically, caught it from the air.

Mom coughed. "Hang on. Where can we find a seamstress who will take on a job like that? It's a lot of work, and there's not much time left."

Kitty held up a hand like a pupil in school. "I'm good with needle and thread. I can do it."

Sisley clapped her hands. "Really, Kitty?"

"Yes." Her aunt smiled back. "I'm in the business, remember? I knew how to sew long before I designed my first hat. I got you, darling."

"Thank you! All of you." Sisley lifted her skirt high and walked around, giving Mom, Amelie, and Sunny a kiss on the top of their heads before she also pressed one into Kitty's curls. It was a first, but Kitty took it in stride.

"We better start soon." Kitty rose. "I need to take my groceries home, but you can bring the dresses over tomorrow around ten."

"You could do it here if you want more space," Mom offered quickly. "You can use your old room as an atelier."

"Thank you. I'll keep it in mind."

"Oh, there's plenty of space here too! I already claimed the guest room upstairs, so Bennett won't walk in and see the dresses!" Sisley replied. Kitty's apartment was so tinyand she didn't seem excited about Mom's spare bedroom.

But Kitty didn't seem to want Sisley's empty room, either. "Let's try it at mine. It's where I have all my sewing supplies."

"Okay."

Mom rose as well. "You're leaving already?"

Kitty moved toward the door. "I have frozen stuff in the trunk. I stood so long at the register the salmonellae are probably dancing a conga line on the chicken."

"I'll call you," Sisley said. "Thanks for coming! And for offering to help."

The blue eyes twinkled from the entry. "Sorry I missed most of it." Kitty waved, and then she slipped on her shoes and let herself out.

Mela clapped her hands suddenly. "Let's pack up the dresses so we don't spill coffee on them! Who wants apple strudel? Sunny made it this morning, and it's de-li-cious. Can you smell it?"

Everybody could smell the warm aroma of vanilla and cinnamon and apple and got up to help cut the strudel and distribute cake plates and forks. Sisley hurried to change. On the way, she caught Mom murmuring to Amelie that Kitty didn't have a freezer in the new apartment.

She locked the bathroom and wiggled out of Julie's dress.

Just because she bought frozen chicken didn't mean Kitty needed a freezer. She could have been planning on cooking it right away. There was no need to come up with a weird excuse to leave, was there?

Sisley slipped her robe back on and hung up the dress. She and Kitty would have long sewing sessions together.

It'd be good to learn more about her aunt.

Chapter 4

"I told her to buy first class. I *told* her that. Just like I told her I didn't do it. She completely misunderstood the text I sent her."

"Yes." Kitty stepped from one foot to the other. The morning breeze blowing through her knitted sweater on the hour-long beach walk had cooled her down. She wanted a cup of hot coffee to warm up again. She also desperately needed to use the restroom.

Plus, she'd forgotten the details of part one through five of her young landlord's story and didn't want him to know. His feelings were already rubbed raw.

All Kitty could remember was that Kevin didn't seem as innocent as he made himself out. Immediately after breaking up with him, his ex had taken off on a backpacking trip to Europe. While he was still denying his new reality, the young lady was solidly moving on. But Kitty wasn't going to break it to him.

Kevin ran a hand through his sandy hair. "Don't you think I'm right?"

Kitty softened at the despair in his eyes. "I think it doesn't matter," she answered. "It doesn't matter so much who's right and who's wrong. Think about yourself now. Maybe it'd be best if you let it go."

"You say it like it's so easy."

"Or don't," she offered. "But I kind of have to..." She exhaled and pointed up the stairs.

"Oh. Sorry." He stepped aside, gesturing for her to proceed.

"Thanks." Kitty hurried up the stairs and let herself in, then softly closed the door. Why, she didn't know. Maybe she was afraid Kevin would burst in to talk more about his relationship? Maybe if Kitty felt better, she'd be okay to listen. He was nice enough, and his friends were all in college or had jobs elsewhere. Everyone needed a shoulder to cry on sometimes.

She locked the door and went into the kitchen.

After the rain of the previous week, the sun was shining. Even Kitty's little roof windows let in enough to give the apartment some cheer. She kicked off her loafers and went to the bathroom, then dug in the pockets of her windbreaker for the sea glass and the sand dollars she'd found. In the kitchen, she washed them and set them on the back of the stove to dry, then made herself coffee.

Steaming mug in hand, she went into the bedroom and sat cross-legged on the bed. Her laptop was waiting, the screen already open. "Okay," she murmured and hit enter.

The funeral and her night of mourning were over. Now she had to start over. She was fifty-five, with a lifetime of experience in starting over under her belt.

The only difference between now and before was money. In her teens and her twenties, it hadn't been so important. She had always been able to catch a gig here or there if she needed a boost. Sewing at first. Later, making hats had crystallized into a living.

It'd been enough while she was living rent-free in Seal Harbor until her bungalow's ancient septic broke. The town took notice, and Kitty had been forced to sell since she couldn't afford to bring the place up to code. Her small online shop and selling at farmers markets were no longer enough to get her through.

After crying her eyes out after the funeral, she rummaged through her boxes until she found an empty notebook. Just a cheap one, like they sell them for cents at the supermarkets after the get-back-to-school time was over.

Kitty had made a list of her goals. First and foremost was a house of her own. After living on her own terms for so long, she couldn't move back to rented apartments or houses where she wasn't allowed to plant in the garden or paint the walls.

It was a lofty goal for someone who was old and broke, but Kitty wanted a place of her own.

The second bullet point on her list said money. Kitty wanted more money. Insurance was costly, and in the back of her mind lived the fear that she might get sick and would need to pay large hospital bills. She liked being fifty-five. She had none of the angst that came with being young and having to find your way. Kitty knew what she wanted and was happy to be herself most of the time. But she also knew her time for living hand-to-mouth was running out.

Kitty touched the keyboard, and the computer screen flickered to life, showing her email inbox. She leaned forward to see what was new—an email from a British lady who had been over-the-moon excited to get an invitation to the Windsor enclosure at the Royal Ascot Race.

As a surprise for her three grown daughters and two best friends, the client had ordered lavish hats for all. The order was not yet paid, but Kitty, eager to show off her hats at the most hatty event of the year, had already ordered materials—best of the best for this showcase opportunity—and spent hours sketching designs so the hats would be ready in time.

The email contained only a few lines, not enough to talk shop. Kitty's insides stilled, and her eyes flew over the short sentences. Regrets, but the client had learned that the Windsor enclosure didn't require hats after all. The daughters, feeling silly, were not going to wear hats—at all, ever. One friend already loved another hat, and the second friend had proved herself unworthy of a custom-made hat by never getting back to the client.

Sorely disappointed, the client would simply wear her mother's old fascinator. Or nothing. Maybe a kerchief, like her Royal Highness wore when it rained. The client hadn't decided but said to go ahead and cancel all orders. Maybe next year, when her family and friends had been to their first race and knew better.

Maybe next year.

Slowly, Kitty closed the laptop. Then she blew out a tight breath through pursed lips, her mind racing like an Ascot horse.

She had a couple of other orders. One for a custom-fit beret and one for a fedora.

It was hardly enough to buy a house. Or get through the summer.

Kitty had to come up with a new plan.

A knock on the door startled her out of her petrified state. She quickly checked the time—almost ten a.m. "Sisley," Kitty murmured. Balancing her coffee, she uncurled and went to open the door.

"Good morning, honey. Come in." Kitty ran a hand through her brown curls. She'd not looked in a mirror since returning from her windswept walk. Her fingers got stuck in a knot, and she flinched as she ripped through it.

"Are you okay?" Her niece's smile slipped. A stuffed dress bag was slung over her shoulder, and the two other dresses hung from her arm. Her cheeks were flushed with exertion, clashing with her blonde hair.

"Of course I am. Where's your baby?"

"Bennett's taken Lovie to the beach," Sisley reported as she squeezed past Kitty into the narrow entry. "She walked twenty steps in a row! And even then, she only stopped because she'd reached her dad. She could've done more. I wish you could see her do it. It's so cute."

Kitty closed the door and unburdened Sisley of the dress bag. "I can't wait to catch her at it. Come through here." She led the way.

"First time I'm here," Sisley noted and craned her neck to look into the kitchen. "I had an apartment under the roof too before I came to Bay Harbor."

"Did you?" Kitty didn't particularly want to talk about this place. Nothing about it was *her*. It was a new feeling because she'd loved her little bungalow in Seal Harbor and never wasted a thought on what guests thought of it. Or her.

"Oh, but..." Sisley stopped at the door to the bedroom. "This is your bedroom, Kitty."

"I know. It's all right." Kitty waved her on as if she didn't mind having her bed covered in fabric and thread and lost needles. "In you go. It's where I'll be doing my hats too."

"Auntie." Her niece turned around. "Kitty."

Kitty tucked her chin in surprise. Sisley had never called her auntie. "What?"

"Sewing three dresses together is going to be such a mess. You'll have to clean up every time you want to take a nap." Sisley's eyes went to the laptop and back. "I have a big old room you can use. It's *empty*. I swear it's not an inconvenience if we do it there. I'll help you bring your sewing things over. We can put up Mom's folding tables. It would be so convenient for you."

Kitty smiled. "But if I do it here, I can work on it at night when I can't sleep." She looked around. "Don't mind the boxes. It's not as bad as it looks."

"I don't mind the boxes. I mind claiming your bedroom on top of you doing me a huge favor. In fact..." Sisley moistened her lips. "I talked with Bennett, and we both agree that we would like to pay you for the alterations. It's a big job."

"No." The word came like a knee-jerk reflex. "Are you kidding me? I don't even want to hear about that." Warmth shot into her cheeks. Did her sister's family pity her so much they wouldn't even let Kitty help prepare her niece for the wedding? Sewing the dress was the only gift Kitty could give. She turned away as shame and exhaustion washed over her like a black wave. "Forget it, Sisley."

"Sorry." Sisley's voice had shrunk. "It's only because I know how expensive it'd be to hire someone for this."

Staring at the door, Kitty counted to three before she turned back. "It's my wedding gift to you. That's all I can give at the moment."

"I'm sorry." Sisley's eyelids fluttered as if she was blinking away invisible tears. "It's a beautiful present. Thank you, Kitty." A stray lock fell in her face.

Kitty reached out and tucked it back. She liked all the young women in Mela's family. But Sisley was her favorite. "If you wore hats, I would make you a trilby," she said quietly. "But you don't wear hats. At least I want to make a dress that makes my niece happy."

"I didn't understand. But now I do." Sisley looked up. "I really appreciate your help. I didn't mean to offend you. I'm sorry."

"No need to apologize." Kitty sighed. "I've had a piece of unwelcome news. Nothing important, but it caught me on the wrong foot." She had to explain her sour reaction. "*I'm* sorry I snapped at you." She went to the boxes and pulled out a sewing basket and a box with scissors and measuring tapes. Then she smiled at her niece. "Let's go use your room, okay?"

"Yes!" Sisley's voice perked up. "It'll be so much easier to spread out the dresses for cutting them up."

Without further ado, Kitty threw her sewing supplies in a tote bag and slipped her anorak and shoes back on. They left, dresses slung over their shoulders, and soon they were in Sisley's pretty ocean-view house with its white fireplaces and big windows and sun-warmed wide-plank wood floors.

The upstairs room, spacious and golden-bright to see seams and hems, truly was empty. Sisley shoved a couple of soft armchairs in and set a one-legged side table in between. While Kitty unzipped the dress bags, Sisley left one more time to fetch a small vase full of wildflowers for the side table, two glasses of champagne, and a plate with pastel-colored macarons.

Kitty watched her gleeful preparations from the corner of her eyes, more thankful with every passing moment that she hadn't insisted on her dim bedroom plan. Of course this was how a wedding dress fitting should be. Beautiful, delicious, sunny. Smelling of macarons the colors of roses and lilac.

"Come help me," Kitty invited her when Sisley was done making the room all it should be.

They spread the dresses on the floor, pulling them together and apart as they decided what should go where. Then Kitty measured Sisley, and when Bennett returned with the baby from the playground, he pretended not to know what they were doing and that he would come in. Sisley in turn pretended to be shocked over it, all to make Lovie break into bubbly peals of laughter again and again until they were all laughing at Lovie's delight.

Sisley then let Lovie join them in the room while Bennett was dispatched with car and keys to fetch Kitty's sewing machine and the dress form and several other things that were necessary and easy enough to find.

Later, Amelie dropped off a platter of assorted sandwiches on artisanal breads, some with delicate cucumber slices, others with cream cheese and salmon. Bennett prepared poached pears with champagne and rose petals to follow up the light lunch, claiming if his mother hadn't forced him, he'd have made a more manly desert.

Kitty saw his eyes when he handed his beloved her glass bowl and didn't believe a word he said. She was sure he would bury his Sisley in rose petals if he could.

She claimed to need quiet to focus on setting everything up and drawing a bit of a pattern to give the lovers some space. By the time Sisley demanded to come back in and help, the room was set up and Kitty had made the first cuts.

"You need more light." Sisley flipped the switch and closed the door behind her.

"Is it this late already?" Kitty glanced out the window. The sun was sinking to meet a pale, rising moon. The bright blue of the sky had turned the soft color of the windswept wild beach roses that grew on the cliffs.

To be honest, Kitty would have liked to stay. Here was something she could do and do well. "I should get back." She patted the loose threads and bits of fabric off her lap.

The little family was settling in for the night. Kitty had lived with Mela long enough to know that it was time for Lovie's bath and goodnight story. The aroma of melting cheese and fresh basil wafting through the house meant Bennett was preparing dinner. Soon, Sisley would be busy running from bath to nursery to kitchen and back.

"I'm so excited about this dress."

"Me too." Kitty rose from the soft armchair.

"Sis? Can you come down for a moment?" Bennett called from downstairs, and then Lovie wailed in protest.

Sisley turned, her hand already on the door handle. "Stay for dinner?"

Kitty smiled and shook her head. "Go ahead, sounds like your baby needs her mama. I'll let myself out."

As if on cue, Lovie wailed again, sounding tired and fed up with having to do without her mother.

"Okay." Sisley slipped out. Kitty cleaned up a little and left. She walked home via Main Street, mulling over the dress and how to best attach one to the other. Lost in thought, she stopped by the small market to buy a packet of bubble-bath salts and a bottle of white wine.

Only when she climbed the stairs did she remember that there still was no bathtub in the apartment. There never would be.

That had been the old place.

She set the bath salts next to the sand dollars on the back of the stove and opened the bottle.

New beginnings were like that. Chaotic, difficult.

Kitty knew chaos. Growing up with a beloved but mentally ill mother and no family support to guide her, she'd done difficult before.

She knew so much more now than back then.

She could do it again.

Wine glass in hand, she opened the laptop and logged into her website.

Chapter 5

"I'm so glad she agreed to do it at my house. But I can tell she really doesn't like relying on other people." Sisley shaded her eyes against the noon sun. They had parked at the harbor, and the light glittered on the blue waves. The temperature was perfect for Sisley's T-shirt and jeans outfit. It would have been perfect for one of her beloved loose hippie dresses as well, but Sisley was ready to tackle some dust and heavy lifting.

"We literally have no use for the spare bedroom." Bennett lifted Lovie out of the car seat, and Sisley squinted at them. Lovie was almost a year old. She was also round, happy, and a daddy's girl. Bennett sat her in the crook of his arm and cradled her while she held on to him in a well-practiced routine. Her big blue eyes checked on Sisley's, making sure Mama was there, and then she looked curiously around.

"Dada."

It was her word for Bennett but also for everything else. Lovie was early with walking and teething but not with talking. Dada seemed to be all she considered necessary.

"Yes, Dada," Sisley confirmed. "That's the sea. Can you say sea, sweetheart?"

Lovie's throat worked. "Dsa."

"You're such a smart girl!" Bennett beamed. "Did you hear her, Sis? She said sea!"

Sisley laughed and pulled her purse from the car before closing the door. The sun was pouring liquid gold over the tiny parking lot by the harbor. Dandelions bloomed in the cracks of the weathered asphalt, and the air carried the scent of driftwood and kelp. "I'm glad you could take off today."

"Me too. So, where is it exactly? I've seen the building before, but it was in one of the little side streets I never use." Lovie had snuggled up to him, her small arm spread over his chest as if she wanted to wrap around him.

"This way." Sisley pulled out her phone to open the map app. "That's Johanna's car over there. And that's Kimmy. They're waiting for us."

"Not our fault that someone kicked their shoes under the sofa." Bennett tickled Lovie's neck, and she giggled. "Is Pippa there?"

"I think so." Pippa was Travis and Kimmie's five-year-old. Well, really, she belonged to Travis. But Sisley wouldn't like to see her sister's face if someone dared to suggest Pippa didn't belong to her too. They'd all fallen hook and sinker for the little girl.

"How about Sunny?" Bennett asked.

"She had something to do with pies today. She's meeting with Mom's particular friend Valerie today."

"Ah, yes, Valerie. I've heard that name. She's my mom's particular friend as well."

He held out his free hand, and Sisley took it. They started walking along the water.

On the waves bobbed a small handful of fishing trawlers and lobster boats but also other, much fancier vessels.

"Look at the beautiful sailboats." Sisley pointed at a pretty one. Golden honey wood gleamed beside the peeling hull of a shabby fisher.

Bennett whistled through his teeth. "Looks like a wallet in the water, if you ask me. I've never seen them before. Not here, anyway. More like Seal Harbor or Bay Port."

"Ever since the motel was renovated, there's been an influx of money into Bay Harbor," Sisley declared, satisfied. "Two more restaurants opened. Peter says the motel is just getting going too. Suddenly they have their hands full."

"Dad has the golden touch." Bennett followed as Sisley turned into Bay View Street. "Whatever he takes on turns a profit. Even I got a promotion since he came back. Hopefully he didn't pay off the chief." He chuckled at the thought.

"I don't think so." Sisley grinned too. Bennett's boss was as hard-boiled as they came. He would arrest someone for even thinking about bribes near him.

"Pretty little cobbled street," Bennett mentioned. "Must be one of the first ones they built here."

The houses of Bay View Street were small fishing cottages with modest front porches and a sliver of grass at the sides leading to a private backyard. The faded picket fences around the small yards lovingly supported brilliant day lilies and nodding peonies. Here and there, a late pear tree or crabapple was in flower.

Sisley pointed at the only tall building. "This is it."

"My word." Bennett's head sank into his neck as he squinted at the proudly pointed Clyde. "A new coat of paint isn't going to do it."

"I told you it was big." Sisley tucked the phone into her bag and looked up and down the empty street. It was only them and the flowers in the sun-flooded front yards. "Who'd have thought there's an old library in this quaint little street, right?"

"Maybe that's why it shut its doors? People couldn't find it?" Bennett shook his head, and just then, Lovie started to swat at his chin for attention.

"Dada. Daaa." She pointed.

"She wants to go to the swing set by the marina," Sisley said. "I told you. Why don't you take her, and we'll meet afterward for an ice cream?"

Bennett liked showing off Lovie at the playground. As the resident homicide detective, people could be shy of him, and his imposing figure didn't make it better. But when he had Lovie with him, in her fluffy headbands and cute little dresses, people liked to take the opportunity to connect. Everyone wanted to know if he had stories, and Bennett readily shared a special feel-good selection he curated for the purpose.

"Okay," he agreed now. "Are you sure you'll be safe in there?"

"Safer than I'd be if I had Lovie with me," Sisley declared. "What if the chandelier falls and I wasn't paying attention?"

"Why? Is the chandelier loose?" Bennett eyed her critically. "Then you shouldn't go in there at all."

Sisley reached out and laid a hand on Bennett's cheek because she wanted to feel his skin, his warmth, that he was real.

"I love you," she said quietly and sincerely. "The chandelier is fine. I'll be fine. I just don't think it is babyproof. Have fun at the playground. I'll text you when I'm done."

Bennett nodded, leaned in and pressed a kiss on her forehead, then lifted Lovie so she too could smack a wet one on her mother's cheek. "Make sure you stay safe. We need you." He left, turning back when he reached the corner to see if she was still standing there.

She waved and he nodded. Then her little family was gone from sight, and she returned her attention to the old library.

It was a white two-story house that stood out from the faded gray-brown shingle houses to its sides. The upper level had a large octagonal window. It was high enough to look out at the sea over the roofs. Squinting up, Sisley glimpsed the glittering reflection of the crystal chandelier dance across the dusty glass of the window. It was such a fairytale sight; her heart quickened with anticipation. All this was theirs?

"Leave it to Morris," she whispered. Her brother had found the place on a midnight walk, ferreted out who owned it, and charmed them into selling the old library to him and Sisley. He'd called the night before to let her know it was theirs.

The white door opened, and there he stood. A boyish grin on his face, his hair tousled. A single cobweb draped over his shoulder, delicate as silk on his black turtleneck sweater.

"Everybody else is here already. I was just coming to prop the door open for you. The doorbell doesn't work. Nothing works, in fact." He grinned and stepped outside, pushing his hands into the pocket of his jeans and joining her in gazing up at the Clyde. It was the first time they were here together after making the purchase. "Well, what do you think?"

Sisley was suddenly overcome with emotion and swallowed. For a penniless girl, it was unreal to have made it this far. And they still had to take it a lot farther. Sometimes, the responsibility felt like she would buckle and get crushed. And yet it was a fairytale come true at the same time. "I honestly don't know," she said faintly. "I love it. I'm scared I can't pull my weight. I've never sold a single painting."

Morris looked at her, his eyebrows raised in surprise. When he saw her face, he put his arm over her shoulder, then pulled her closer. "But do you like it, little sister?" he asked, the boyish grin making its way into his voice.

"It is fantastic," Sisley got out. "I can't believe we'll work here."

"And yet we will," Morris replied. "Every once in a while, even artists get lucky."

Sisley leaned her head onto his shoulder. "But I'm not an artist," she said. "Only you are. For years, you have paid the bills playing your piano. You know what you can do. I have done nothing yet to earn the title."

His body vibrated with quiet laughter. "If your paintings could talk, they'd beg to differ."

"Is that how it works?" She smiled.

He nodded. "If you create, you're an artist. Full stop. Like I said, it helps to get lucky now and then."

"How exactly did you talk the owner into selling it?"

"You mean, how did I talk the owner of the library into gifting it to us?" Morris sighed. "He's in hospice. His heirs were the nicest people, but they're already wealthy and busy and don't want to bother with some falling-down place in Bay Harbor. They need neither the money nor the hassle. It was ours for the asking."

"No conditions?" Sisley couldn't help but think there was more to the story than Morris shared.

"Well." He let go of her and straightened. "We have to use it for the arts, and we'll have to pay the tax. And we have to figure out what to do with all the books."

"The books are still in there? It really, truly was a library?"

"It was a private library," he confirmed. "And the books are still in there. I thought we'd keep a few in the built-in shelves and give away what we can. The rest—don't know. We'll figure it out."

"There are built-in shelves?" Sisley asked weakly. "Is it gorgeous?"

He let go and pushed the door open. "It is gorgeous." He gestured for her to go inside. "You have no idea *how* gorgeous it is. Come on in. I want to see your face when you see the hall."

Chapter 6

The book slipped from Kimmie's fingers and dropped into the box. "Oops." She lifted it out and made sure the pages lay flat between the leather-bound covers. "That one was heavy."

She set it down carefully and straightened her back. There it was again, that twinge. Weird. Never in her life had her lower back given her trouble. She rubbed the spot to make it go away.

Travis, high up on the library ladder, returned the next volume to the shelf. "Are you tired?"

"I am, actually," Kimmie answered.

"You slept in," he noted. "And it's barely ten. Did you have breakfast at your Mom's?"

"I sat down with Pippa while she ate," Kimmie replied and shook out her hand. "But I didn't have an appetite." She looked up at him. "It seems I can't stand the smell of bacon anymore."

"You love bacon."

"Apparently not."

His eyes met hers, and an unspoken thought passed between them. He took a step down. "Are you hungry now? You ought to be since you haven't had anything."

"My stomach is rumbling. But nothing sounds good."

"Your favorite clam chowder?" he tempted her and took another rung. "Something hot and creamy?"

Kimmie shifted restlessly on her feet. Just the thought made her want to run away. "No. Ugh." Suddenly, a wave of nausea rolled over her. "Travis."

"Yes?"

"I feel sick. I might have to throw up."

"Right. Okay." He climbed down to where she stood. He took her hands in his. "Sick as in you have the flu, or sick as in...?"

Kimmie inhaled the clean, salty air coming in from the window. She could feel small beads of sweat form on her temples. "I've never had the flu in June. And I have no experience in the second option." She gulped a breath. "But possibly it's that one."

Travis's chest rose and sank, and then he stepped so close she had to look up to see his eyes. "Really?" he whispered.

"I know it was a false alarm before." She smiled weakly. Right after their first time, she thought she felt wonky. But it had turned out to be nerves at being back together with her one true love. This was nothing like that. This was real.

"Is it different from before?" He held her gaze.

"It's very different now," she agreed. "That doesn't mean I can tell how it feels when you're...you know." She delicately trailed off. She didn't want to say the word.

Pregnant.

She hadn't planned on being pregnant. Pretty sure Travis hadn't planned on it. They weren't as careful as they should be...but they weren't exactly careless, either. And Kimmie had an appointment to get a birth control prescription for two months. The nearest doctor was in Sandville and booked half a year ahead.

"Do you need to throw up?"

She checked in with her belly. "It's a bit better right now."

"Let's go, Kimmie." He put an arm around her and started walking.

She followed him through the piles of books. "Where to?"

"The store." He waved at Johanna, who was on the other side of the hall. Johanna had a bandanna wrapped over her mouth and nose like a bandit so she wouldn't swallow the dust swirling off the old books. She gave a thumbs-up back.

They'd taken turns going to lunch in groups of two and threes. Somebody was always plugging away at filling the book boxes or labeling them for their destination.

Once they were outside on Bay View, they both brushed off their shirts and inhaled the fresh air. Then Travis held out his hand again.

Kimmie took it, and they started toward Main Street. The tiny mom-and-pop grocer sold two or three brands of pregnancy tests. Kimmie had glanced at them the day before after putting butter and jam in her shopping basket made her feel nauseated. She ended up not buying a test because it couldn't be real, could it? There were other bugs in the air than the flu. Or maybe there was mold in the library?

The look on Travis's face as he opened the door to the store made it a lot more real. He squeezed her hand. "Don't worry. It'll be all right."

"What if...oh." Kimmie pressed her lips together. Another wave of nausea rolled over, this one strong enough she didn't trust herself to finish the sentence.

"Uh-oh." Travis rubbed his chin, his three-day beard scrunching under his palm. "Better stay on the bench out here, honey. I'll be back in two."

"Last aisle to the right," Kimmie got out before she sank onto the small blue bench nearby.

"Got it." He disappeared, the little bell clinging brightly as the door fell shut behind him.

Kimmy whimpered softly into her hands. "I feel *sick*."

"Oh dear," an old voice replied.

Kimmie looked up. One of the old ladies from the senior canasta club peered around the store's stack of firewood, choosing a bundle. "I should probably go home," Kimmie said miserably. "Sorry."

"Do you want me to call your mom to come and pick you up?" the old lady asked.

Lots of the older people still remembered Kimmie's grandmother Julie and had reconnected with 'little Mela' since she returned to Bay Harbor. Even if Kimmie and her siblings didn't know everyone in town by name, they seemed to know them.

"I'm waiting for my..." For her what? Travis wasn't her husband anymore because they'd gotten divorced two years before. Calling him her boyfriend didn't seem right, either.

"Your significant other?" the old lady suggested delicately.

Kimmie nodded. Somehow, talking to the lady made her feel better.

"He's buying milk while you sit out here feeling sick?" She cocked her head as if she was going to march into the store to give Travis a piece of her mind.

"He's not buying milk," Kimmie said. "He's in there *because* I feel sick." She nodded at her belly.

"Oh." The lady's eyes widened as if she'd figured it out. "Oh!"

Kimmie shrugged. "It may be nothing but a stomach bug after all."

A smile appeared on the old lady's face, and she moved closer. "I hope for your sake it's the good kind of stomach bug." She sat down beside Kimmie. "I'm Alice Harper, by the way. I make for an excellent babysitter."

Kimmie was pursing her lips, but Alice Harper held up a hand.

"Ah! Ta-ta-ta! Never reject the offer of a babysitter. I know you have your whole family to help out, but there always comes a time when everybody has enough to do already. And I ran a preschool for thirty years. I'm the best of the best when it comes to reading to little kids."

"Oh, I see," Kimmie said. "Now it makes sense."

Alice Harper patted Kimmie's knee. "Truth be told, I miss it. I never had kids of my own, but I miss all my little students. I can remember every single one of them. Isn't that funny? So many of them, and I can still tell you who never needed a diaper, who shared their toys without prompting, and who ate their cookies the fastest."

"Wow." Kimmie smiled. "Where can I find you if, in two to three years, I might need a babysitter?"

"Around Bay Harbor, I sincerely hope." Alice smiled back. "Especially on Arbor Street. The yellow house is mine. There's only one. Well...good luck, Kimmie."

"Thank you," Kimmie replied. She liked Alice Harper, and it was a sweet offer to read to the baby she was maybe carrying. "Don't tell Mom about this. I don't even know that it's not a stomach bug."

"It's not. But I won't tell little Mela."

The answer had come quickly. Bay Harbor was small, and gossip kindled as easily as a beach bonfire on a midsummer night. Kimmie tucked her chin. "Don't tell anyone else either?"

This time, the answer came slower. "Fine," Alice promised finally. "But you let me know next time we meet."

Kimmie smiled. "Fine," she agreed back. Her stomach had settled, and she stood and held out her hand. "Nice to meet you, Alice Harper. I'm Kimmie."

The beautiful, wrinkled face folded into a wide smile. For the flash of a moment, Kimmie saw the hundreds and hundreds of children's eyes that had watched Alice's face over the years, waiting for that smile because it meant the world to them.

"Nice to meet you too, Kimmie," Alice replied.

"Wait." Kimmie hesitated. "I have a little...um..." What was Pippa, Travis's daughter, to her? She didn't have a term for it any more than for Travis. The five-year-old wasn't a stepchild nor her daughter. "I already have a little girl at home," Kimmie said in the end. "Her name is Pippa. If you're willing to read to *her* sometimes, she would love it. She also has a little friend, Brooke. She's younger, but she's incredibly smart and loves books. Maybe you could come meet the kids sometime soon? Maybe Monday in the afternoon?"

Alice's smile faltered for a moment. Then she nodded solemnly. "I can do Monday. I could read them a book about flowers that was a favorite of my school kids. We could look at flowers in the yard afterward."

"That sounds great. They certainly won't learn anything about flowers from me."

The old lady nodded, and then she waved goodbye, lifted a bundle of wood from the stack, and stepped into the store. Travis passed her on his way out.

"Who was that?" he asked.

"Alice Harper. She used to teach preschool, and she'll come to read to Pippa and Brooke on Monday."

Travis raised an eyebrow. "You know her?"

"I'll get to know her," Kimmie said. "I'll be there with them." She pointed at the small paper bag under his arm. "Did you find one?"

"Yes. I swear the girl at the register stared at it for the longest time. The price tag was right there. All she needed to do was ring it up." He shook his head. "Brace yourself. I think the gossip mill is already churning."

Kimmie put a hand on his arm. "It's a small town. Hey. I feel better."

"No more nausea?"

"No. Perfectly well." The nausea had left suddenly and completely. Like she'd felt a twinge in her back before, Kimmie now felt a slight but definite twinge of disappointment. "It's gone. I'm even hungry." She laughed, embarrassed. "Gosh, maybe I was just dehydrated after all. Sorry for making a fuss, Travis."

"Well." He tucked the small paper bag under his arm and ran a hand through his hair. "The fact that it's gone completely actually means it's not dehydration. Unless you drank water while I was inside?"

"No."

"Don't be scared." He took her into his arms and hugged her to him even though more people were passing them on their way to the store. "Let's go test, okay?"

His breath tickled her ear. She closed her eyes for a moment. When she opened them again, her heart beat to a new rhythm.

He was right. She had been scared. But she wanted this. If the test was negative, she would feel crushed. "Okay," she murmured.

Hand in hand, they walked back to the old library.

The downstairs ladies' powder room was unnecessarily spacious, with a dusty round velvet bench the shape of a Bundt cake. It was surrounded by gilded mirrors that were foggy with age and had thin, branching cracks like quicksilver cobwebs.

"I'll wait here." Travis handed her the paper bag and sat on the bench.

At least peeing on a stick wasn't a problem. Kimmie always had to pee now.

A few moments later, Kimmie came out of the stall, test in hand. She sat beside Travis. "Three minutes," she said. "We have to wait for three minutes."

"The longest three minutes in the history of humanity." He put an arm around her shoulders and pulled her back until they both rested their heads against the raised middle, staring at the stucco medallion on the ceiling.

"Three minutes." His voice was carefully neutral.

Kimmie thought they had years to sort out things between them. Now it came down to one hundred eighty seconds. One hundred sixty seconds. Fifty.

"What if it's positive, Travis?" Kimmie turned her head just enough to see her man from the corner of her eye. He'd left her before, divorcing her without a word of explanation. "What will you do if I'm pregnant?"

Chapter 7

"There must be a mistake, ma'am." The freckled teenager at the register glanced at the credit card. "It's not accepting it." She handed the card back. Carefully, with a small supportive smile, as if she knew the feeling in Kitty's chest.

"I'm sorry." Kitty hastily tucked the credit card into her wallet. "If I can put the oatmeal back, I'll have enough to pay cash. And...maybe the hair shampoo."

"Of course." The girl set the things aside and tapped some keys. "Twenty-four seventeen, then."

Kitty pulled the last twenty and a five-dollar bill from her wallet and handed them over. Her cheeks felt like embers, ready to spark fire. "Thanks," she murmured, taking her penny change and paper bag.

"Sure." The teen smiled. "Do you need help with that?"

The bag of groceries in Kitty's arm was much too small to warrant the question. It was a sign of good will, not an offer to carry the bag. Kitty tried to smile. "I'm good. Thanks."

The teen turned back to her phone. "See you soon," she said casually.

Kitty left quickly and quietly, glad there'd been nobody else waiting in line behind her and following the exchange. Outside, she filled her lungs again with the fresh air.

Kimmie and Travis were walking away from the market, cuddled into each other's arms.

Kitty hitched her bag higher and set off for her apartment.

The charges for the Ascot hat supplies must've gone through. That's why her card was suddenly maxed out. Kitty stepped on a wooden bridge that spanned a tiny but determined creek between the market and Main Street. When she leaned over the side, a white duck with a huddle of fluffy yellow ducklings looked up at her, paddling on the spot.

Kitty smiled. She wasn't the only one trying to make things work. "Here you go." She broke off the end of her loaf of sourdough bread and crumbled it into the water. "It's probably not what you should be eating. But in a pinch, it's better than nothing."

The duck snattered her bill through the water to catch the crumbs before the creek carried them to the sea, and the ducklings eagerly followed her example.

Kitty watched for a while. Then she walked home, taking the long path by the harbor to air out her thoughts. It was hard to feel bad on an early June afternoon in Bay Harbor. How many people would give their last dime to change places with her?

Maybe nobody. But she would.

Kitty broke off another morsel for a hungry gull and hurried on before the gull's sharp-eyed cousins caught on to the feast.

Clients canceled orders all the time. Sometimes, Kitty doubted they even knew there was a real person at the other end of the transaction. A person who had to pay upfront for supplies and who spent hours making the ordered hat.

Safely out of reach of the squawking gulls, Kitty stopped to admire the boats.

She needed only one happy customer to get started again. Someone who told her friends who told their friends. Jaunty fascinators, elegant cloches, gorgeous wide-brim hats...she could make them all.

Once, years ago, Kitty had gotten an order for twenty pirate hats for a group of friends going to a Renaissance fair. That could happen again too.

Kitty turned away from the harbor and climbed up the steep end of her street.

She'd buckle down and get back to business. Things would turn out okay. She wouldn't allow herself to believe otherwise.

She let herself in and tiptoed upstairs so her landlord, Kevin, wouldn't catch her to tell her the next installment of his ex-girlfriend's adventures. She could barely deal with the complications in her own life right now.

When she climbed the stairs, she saw there were several packages waiting by her door. Her landlord must've brought them upstairs, so she didn't have to. Feeling guilty for dodging him, she pushed the boxes inside and softly closed the door behind her.

Unpacking the groceries took only a minute since there wasn't very much, and then she slid a knife through the packing tape and opened the packages.

At least now she had materials to make some great new hats, showstoppers she could use to attract clients and clicks on her website. She had sat up late the previous night, sketching and planning how to revamp her online store. With a bit of luck, she'd only stay in the apartment a year or two...

Kitty glanced at the unused bath salts. She'd have a bathtub again before she turned sixty. She'd wanted so much more when she was younger. Now, a bathtub seemed enough.

One box revealed a bundle of smooth sheets of felt. Kitty lifted it out to admire the quality. Good fedoras were popular at the sea in the summer. She filled her arms with felt and feathers and rolls of hat bands and went into the bedroom to work.

By the time there was a knock on her door, the bright light of the day had started to dim. Kitty looked up from her design sketches and blinked. Where had the hours gone?

She unfolded her legs, groaning when the blood prickled in her toes.

Another knock. "I'm coming!" she called. Brushing snippings of fabric and felt off her sweater, she hobbled to the door and opened it.

"Hi, Kitty." Mela looked at her. She was dressed in an immaculate white linen dress, the narrow straps emphasizing the tan of her skin. Her beach-blonde hair with the first elegant streaks of silver curled at her jawline, and a pair of sunglasses was tucked in the front of the dress. She looked so relaxed and sophisticated at the same time that Kitty cringed.

She was dressed in sweats and an old drugstore sweater with a lobster on it, her short curls escaping the messy ponytail. She should at least have taken a shower.

"Hi, Mela." Kitty picked a thread off her sleeve. Had she forgotten a meeting with her sister?

"Can I come in?" Mela's foot was already in the door.

Kitty stepped aside and gestured a welcome. It was too late now to straighten anything or pretend she was doing better than she was. "Sure." She led the way into the kitchen. "Would you like a cup of tea?"

"If you don't mind." Mela put her oversized straw tote on the ground where it glaringly matched her espadrille wedge. "How are you doing? Everything okay?"

"Yes. How are *you*?" Kitty turned on the faucet to fill the kettle. "How is the motel?"

"The motel is going crazy. I have no idea where all these people are suddenly coming from." Sincerity warmed Mela's voice. "It went from empty to overbooked the moment Maisie and Ellie started recommending us."

Kitty nodded. Maisie and Ellie ran a successful inn in Beach Cove. Their mansion at the sea was beautiful, but it had only a small handful of rooms. They often had to turn away people looking for a room before the Bay Harbor motel was renovated from the ground up. Now, their overflow filled the rooms in Bay

Harbor as well, and the happy guests, excited to share their secret tip, spread the word about the charming town as fast as an octopus spreads ink. It was exactly what Kitty needed to happen for her own business as well.

"Good," she said. "I'm glad."

"Peter and Charlie can barely keep up. In fact, they are holding interviews for staff positions right now." Mela checked the slim gold watch on her arm. "If this keeps going, the motel will become a major employer in Bay Harbor." She smiled. "Who'd have thought, huh?"

"I know!" The stove hissed to life, and Kitty put the kettle on the flame. It smelled of burned bread, and she blew the offending crumb away from the fire. "What else is happening?"

"I was wondering whether you want to sell hats at the farmers market this Saturday? Are you coming? There's plenty of space. Or you can have all the space. I'm almost out of honey, and I won't fill more jars before late summer. I'd hate to have to find someone else to take over the stand until then."

The rule was that no stands could be unoccupied, no matter who owned them. It didn't look good and cost the neighboring sellers if visitors decided to stick to the busier areas. "I might." Kitty got her tea tin and pried off the lid. There wasn't much left. "Earl Grey?"

Mela pulled a bulging plastic bag from her tote. "Sunny sends you some of the sheet cake she baked this morning. And these"—another bag stuffed to the brim appeared—"are peach tarts."

Kitty smiled. It didn't matter now that most of her sourdough loaf had gone to the birds. "Tell Sunny thanks for me."

Mela lifted a tray from the depth of the tote. "You also forgot the lasagna at my house." She set it on the table. "Sunny cut it up and froze the portions. You can slowly defrost it in the fridge and only warm up what you need. It should be good for at least a week like this."

"Oh. How thoughtful."

Mela stood to put the tray into the fridge. "Kitty, don't you have any food in the house?"

The kettle whistled. "I have all I need." Kitty poured the water into the mugs.

"I know, but...you know you're always welcome to come back to Seasweet Lane, don't you?" Mela sat back down.

Kitty set the mugs on the table and joined her sister. "Mela," she said firmly. "I enjoyed staying with you. But two months is enough."

"Why? I love having you. You can move in for good if you like. Seriously."

"You're very generous. But I don't feel right staying with you. Or anyone else, for that matter. If we had grown up together, I would probably feel differently. But we only just met a few months ago."

"I'm glad to have you for a sister," Mela insisted.

"I'm glad to have you for a sister too." Kitty had to smile. "But we're still strangers to each other."

"Oh, we're not strangers after living together for two months." The words didn't sound convincing; there was a waver in Mela's voice that told Kitty she felt the same.

"At least let me help you get on your feet." Mela was dropping all pretense now. She gestured around the kitchen. "I was lucky to have a house to come back to. Let me help you now. You don't need to live like this."

Kitty took a long, slow breath, counting to three on the exhale. "You don't know me at all, dear sister. I'm stubborn. I'm independent. I always have been, even as a child. My father left us. My mother wasn't very, shall we say, motherly? Depending on others makes me nervous. Nervous with a capital N. I can't take it."

"I'm your sister, not your mother. I'm not going to let you down."

Kitty drained her tea as a sign that she was done discussing this. In Seal Harbor, she'd been known as an outstanding hatmaker. Here, she was the poor relative knocking on the door asking favors. It sat even worse with her than the fact that she didn't have a bathtub. "I'll be at the farmers market on Saturday." She carried her cup to the sink. "Tell Sunny thank you."

Mela rose too. Her tea was untouched. "Would you like to go on a beach walk?"

Her sister was generous—and tenacious. "I have to finish some work," Kitty said gently. "Sometime soon, yes. I'd like that."

Mela emptied her mug into the sink and rinsed it. "Then I'll see you Saturday at the market. Oh. Sisley wants me to tell you to go check out the abandoned library she and Johanna and Morris bought."

Sisley had told Kitty about the purchase. Decades before, a wealthy man gifted his wife a library in Bay Harbor, where she grew up poor and without access to books. The wife had died, and the husband was in hospice at home in Nantucket. He sold the building and books to Morris and Sisley, asking only for a song and a handshake and the promise to use the place for the arts.

"I will go and have a look soon," Kitty promised. "I'm curious. Did you see it already?"

"Yes. It's beautiful. Also, falling apart." Mela walked to the door. Her hand on the handle, she turned, determination etched on her face. "You're coming to dinner on Saturday," she ordered. "And lunch on Sunday. The entire family will be there. I'm going to put the table under the apple trees."

"Okay." Kitty's lips twitched at her sister's bossy tone. Kitty wasn't the only one who could put her foot down. More than any promises, it made her warm toward her sister.

"And you're spending the night," Mela went on.

"No, I'm not." Kitty couldn't hold the grin back any longer. "Bye, kiddo."

"Worth a try. At least I got your promise for dinner." Mela opened the door. "By the way, how is the wedding dress coming along?"

"It's all in my head and just needs to be put together."

"Can't wait to see it." Mela left, softly closing the door behind her.

Kitty ran both hands through her hair. Mela was great. Generous, kind, sincere—Kitty couldn't imagine a better sister.

Why, then, did she feel like she was all alone?

Chapter 8

The ocean breeze carried with it the sweet fragrances of fresh seaweed and drying driftwood as Kitty walked along the beach. She carried her sandals in her hand because the sand, grainy and fine beneath her feet, was warm from the sun. But while the land already embraced summer, the water remembered that it was still spring. The sea foam nipped her toes when Kitty stepped into it, and the waves sent a cool morning breeze dancing toward the coast.

It blew Kitty's brown hair into her face and tickled her nose. She tucked the curl back behind her ear; she'd washed her hair that morning, but already it smelled again of Eau de Sunscreen and salt. She stopped for a moment, turning to admire the sea glittering in the sun.

The tide was rising, and the strip of sand she walked on grew slimmer and slimmer. At its highest, the beach roses would hang over the lapping waves. There would always be space to walk here, though; Kitty had been caught by the tide before here. There were spots where she'd had to slosh through the water, but it was never dangerous or more than ankle-deep.

She resumed her walk. This little beach was tame and playful, nothing like the half-crescent-shaped strip of sand over in Beach Cove that had been Dad's favorite beach. His final resting place too. Mela had shown it to Kitty. They'd stood silently, watching the tidal waves slam into the rock. The cliff hid caves and tunnels that never flooded, but by the time the current carried Dad there, it had been too late. His boat capsized far out, and the wild waves claimed him for their own.

Mom, on the other hand, rested in an urn in Kitty's closet. The urn looked as gray and steely as Mom's hand had been before Kitty was fast enough to run and smart enough to dodge. Mom's bad spells never lasted long, but to a small girl, they'd felt dangerous. Several times, Mela had gently asked after Kitty's mom, prodding at her past.

As usual, Kitty delivered the sanitized version. The real memories she kept carefully locked away. Mom had struggled to do her best. Despite everything, despite the gray, the steel, the danger, Kitty would always love her mother.

When the beach ended, Kitty slipped her sandals back on and walked across the harbor parking lot. The gulls squawked as they circled the incoming fish trawlers. Before she turned into Bay View Street, she took a last look at the sea.

Martin used to tell her his stories; like most, they had fished for lobsters and mussels, haddock and halibut and alewife. They swam and dove in the summer and in the winter battled the icy storm waves in their boats. Their lives, their struggles and successes, had been bound to the sea. Long before Kitty was born, her family came to beaches and harbors like these. They had stood watching the water just as the generations following in their wake. Just like Kitty.

Maybe she'd never truly understood until now.

Mela's visit, the shame it fanned in Kitty's chest, had kept her thinking long after while she was pinning fabric and steaming hat bands. It wasn't caused by her humble apartment or the fact she had no money. It was because leaving Seal Harbor and losing Martin made her feel disconnected. And somewhere deep in her heart, she was still that little girl whose own mother couldn't love her back. Who told her that if she was lonely and unloved, it was because she deserved it.

Kitty's shoulders instinctively hunched forward as if her body expected a blow.

A small sound escaped her throat as she cowered. To feel old and poor was difficult. But to feel old and poor and unlovable felt as dangerous as her mother's bad spells.

Kitty closed her eyes. This was her rock bottom.

She opened her eyes again, squinting at the sun glinting off the ripples in the water.

She had the sea. It connected her to generations before her.

Kitty lifted her chin. She wasn't a helpless child anymore. And she wasn't alone. She didn't have to feel lonely.

She'd let old beliefs take over. Mela and her big happy family could not change what was in Kitty's head. She saw that now. She had to climb her way into a happier place herself. But her new family was holding out many helping hands, hoping she'd grab one.

She'd been scared before. Now, she would simply take the hands. She had nowhere to fall if they let go. She'd already hit rock bottom.

Bay Harbor was a place of solace and respite from the world, a place where she could find her own peace. At the end of the pier was a group of fishermen mending their nets. With each stroke of the needle, they were connecting with the past, finding their place in the present, and creating their future.

The tranquil scene before her filled her with a calm that made her pull the salty air into her lungs like a healing elixir.

Without a doubt, Kitty knew that her life would never be the same again, and she felt a renewed sense of purpose. Looking out at the waves, she knew for the first time with absolute certainty that this was the place she belonged.

Everything until now had been preparation, it suddenly felt like. Now was the time for her fresh start. Right now.

She turned to walk on. It wasn't far.

Bay View Street was quiet and peaceful as she walked up the sidewalk. The stones buckled with age and grew yellow dandelions at the edges. June roses spilled over faded fences as crooked and charming as the houses behind. It was barely nine in the morning, but the aroma of cooking wafted in the air. For the first time in a long while, Kitty felt hungry.

As if she had purged the bad memories of her childhood, a happy one came to her. Her mother hadn't always been angry. Sometimes she was generous and caring. She cooked, filling the house with delicious smells from her kitchen. She whipped up feasts that made Kitty's mouth water and filled her belly. Together, they spent time talking and laughing. Kitty cherished those moments when they felt like a family even though she learned quickly that the other shoe would drop soon, the switch would flick back. But she also learned to enjoy her mother's love when it shined on her.

The abandoned library was easy to spot. It was towering over the other buildings, the white paint on the cedar shingles peeling with age. In its heyday, it would have been glorious.

The library's door was sturdy wood, with a circle of glass at the top and smooth brass handles that had been dulled by the salt. Kitty pulled it open and stepped inside.

"Hello?" The air tasted of dust, the dry, old kind that coats the back of the throat, leaving a powdery taste in the mouth.

The door fell shut behind her with a deep thud. Kitty went further into the round hall that opened up before her. It was like stepping into a circus rink of books.

The walls were lined with shelves of carved wood, strewn with ladders to reach even the highest volumes. Some rungs were broken and splintered, their wood warped by neglect, but others seemed intact and called for her to try them out.

Kitty stood in the center of the hall and put her head into her neck. The ceiling rose high above, the details of trim and rosettes lost in the dim sunlight filtering through the salt-coated windows. Keeping her eyes on the chandelier, she turned as if in a dance; it was a magical place. A smile spread over her lips. The hatmaker had entered the arena. Finally. She could almost hear music and laughter.

But there was no audience, and this was no circus. The only magic was the one people caused themselves. Kitty stopped and looked down. Beneath her feet, the floor was tiled in a mosaic pattern of flowers and birds and waves. Even here, the sea kept her company.

"Isn't it gorgeous?"

Chapter 9

Kitty wheeled around. "It is. I had a moment there." She laughed, thinking she must have looked like a loon, swirling on her own in the middle of the hall. But she wasn't embarrassed—it had been too magical. Gone was the gloom of the previous night. Already, deciding that this was her new beginning and that Bay Harbor was her new home felt like the best decision she'd made in a long time. "I'm glad you're here. For a minute, I thought I was the first to get here."

Sisley descended the wooden staircase that wound its way to the second level. "I'm glad you came, Kitty. We're upstairs, boxing up books and cleaning."

Sisley came down the last few steps and joined Kitty in the middle of the hall. She carried with her a mix of salty sea air and sweet beach roses as if she too had just come in from a walk.

"This is going to be the space for concerts and events."

"What about your paintings?" Kitty knew that Sisley had worked hard to get a stock of paintings together. Though she dropped out of art school, she was very talented. The past two months had seen her studying techniques and painting for hours on end.

Sisley pointed over her shoulder at the stairs. "There's another hall upstairs. It has a beautiful window and all the natural light you could ask for. I think we will have the gallery up there. There's also a couple of rooms off to each side that are mostly windows. I'll use one as my studio. I can't wait to show it to you."

"Sounds marvelous. I'm so happy for you." Kitty knew Sisley's path hadn't been easy. "Once the renovations are done, you'll be glad every day you get to work here."

"I'm already glad. In fact, I keep pinching my wrist because it's a dream. I just hope it all works out the way Morris says. I've never sold a painting before."

"But the gallery owner in Sandville said you had potential. He was ready to show your seascapes, wasn't he? Surely that means something." Kitty had been staying at Mela's house when that happened. It'd been big news in Seasweet Lane, and Morris popped a bottle of champagne to celebrate the oracle. They had it out in the field where Sisley had painted the seascapes, wrapped in blankets against the cold while they cheered the waves and the wind.

Her niece nodded and looked up. Clearly, she was worried about pulling her weight in the new venture. "At least we got such a bargain at this library. I can't believe Mr. Brennan just gave it to us." She shook her head, her blonde hair swishing over her shoulders. "Can you fathom anyone being so rich they are able to simply give all this away?"

Kitty had witnessed enough wealth in Seal Harbor to fathom pretty much anything. "In the end, it was probably easiest for him. And if he wanted to see it put to good use—why not? I'm sure you and your brother will do that."

"Come, I'll give you a tour. Take a load of this." Sisley pointed at the chandelier hanging from an ornate ceiling medallion. It was a crystal octagon with a round middle and eight curved points, each dripping with pendants. Somehow, they had repelled the dust and sparkled where the sun hit them, reflecting dancing rays of fractured light on the books.

"I already noticed that one," Kitty said, smiling. "What a beauty. Definitely hard to overlook."

"There's another upstairs. It's made of smaller crystals, but it breaks the light like a prism. I can't understand how Mr. Brennan doesn't want them! I'd never leave them behind." Sisley's hands gesticulated, trying to keep pace with her words. She was as excited as a child at Christmas.

Maybe it hadn't occurred to her niece that Mr. Brennan wouldn't be able to take his pretty chandeliers with him where he was going.

"And look at the furniture! I could never ever afford anything like it. Even Ikea is expensive when you're on my budget." Sisley laughed.

"I know what you mean." Kitty chuckled too, more delighted with her vivacious niece than the antiques.

They strolled around, pacing the size of the hall. In the nooks on either side, Kitty spotted chairs and more small tables made for resting and reading. She wiped the dull dust off one, making the smooth dark wood gleam.

"Did you notice the art? Most are coastal landscapes. But not this one." The walls were hung with golden frames, and Sisley stopped in front of an oil painting.

Kitty joined her. The painting was of a very stern-looking man. His hair looked glued to his head, and his eyebrows and the drop of his lips boded nothing good. He looked like he wanted every person in the library to hush down and study hard. "Mr. Brennan?"

Sisley nodded. "I think so. Of course he was much younger then, but I still recognize him."

"He doesn't look too welcoming."

As if it were the most natural thing in the world, Sisley hooked her arm under Kitty's. "Strange, given how sweet he was when we visited him."

"And that?" Kitty turned. Opposite to stern Mr. Brennan was another portrait. It was much more pleasant to look at, picturing a smiling woman who held a disheveled miniature Schnauzer dog in her lap. The Schnauzer peered through a thick fringe at Mr. Brennan, his stance feisty. Possibly the two had been in a stare-off in real life as well, Kitty thought. Maybe Mr. Brennan's frown was meant for the little rascal, not the visitors to the library.

"That would be the wife, Alisande Brennan. He built the library as a wedding gift to her. She was poor when she grew up. But she was smart and went to university before studying was a thing for women, let alone the daughter of a lobster fisher."

"That can't have been easy."

"You know fishermen." Sisley smiled. "She wasn't faint of heart. She won an award for a bridge design. She'd entered the competition under a male name, but it was the best design they had. In the end, they allowed her to build it. She was the first female architect who built a bridge in Maine."

"She looks happy," Kitty said quietly. "She must have liked her husband. What a thoughtful gift."

"I don't think he ever got over losing her. He still loves her very much," Sisley said. "Who knows? Maybe his portrait was painted before they married. Maybe he had an unhappy childhood."

"Maybe he didn't like her little dog. Schnauzers can be very protective." Unhappy childhood meant different things to different people. For her, it was the unsettling twitch of a muscle in Mom's cheek and a cold kitchen. "But more likely it was simply the way they made him pose back then," she said. "Maybe he was suspicious the painter would fall in love with his lady."

Sisley laughed. "That's silly. She was way too smart to take off with a poor painter when she could build bridges and have her own library. Come, I'll show you the upstairs." She turned away, pulling Kitty with her.

They climbed the winding staircase. Like the furniture, the quality of the wood was solid. Old as the steps and sweeping banister were, there wasn't a single creak or wobble. When Kitty pointed it out, Sisley put a hand to her heart. "I agree. I was so relieved when we found the building structure is good. Vandals broke some of the book ladders before Mr. Brennan's people caught on and fixed the backdoors. But besides the ladders, everything is perfectly fine, which is a huge relief because we don't have to pay for fixing it."

"You'll be all right." The financial burden she took on, gifted building or not, seemed to weigh heavily on her niece. "Trust your brother when he says you can make it work."

The rest of the family was upstairs, greeting them cheerfully and abandoning their cleaning to follow around as Kitty explored the lofty rooms. Like downstairs, there was one large main room too. As promised, it was graced with a huge octagonal window looking over the sea. The glass reached almost from floor to ceiling. If Mrs. Brennan loved the sea that had sustained her family in Bay Harbor, she could have read in front of it without having to worry about the pages of her book getting blown about by the breeze.

"This is where my gallery will be." Sisley opened the door to the left, showing Kitty a room that was smaller but almost as bright. On the wall already hung some of her colorful paintings.

"They look great." Drawn by the cheer of the colors, Kitty went closer. "I really think you can pull this off, my dear. If I had any decent light in my place, I'd buy them all. You certainly deserve an atelier like this."

Sisley rubbed a hand over her cheek. "Feels preposterous to call it my studio, let alone my atelier. I'm no professional—but thank you for your kind words. Morris says to just get going."

"Rule number one for any artist: you gotta do it," her brother confirmed good-humoredly. "You have at least as much talent for painting as I have for making music. I earn a living, so you should be able to do the same. If you keep at it, the rest will come."

"More than anything, I want to believe that's true." Sisley chuckled nervously.

Soon after, Johanna and Kimmie declared they needed chocolate croissants and coffee and left to get them at the Beach Bistro. Travis and Morris returned to pulling books off the shelves that covered the upstairs walls and piling them into boxes. The plan was to remove the shelves so there would be space for hanging artwork.

"Where are the kids?" Kitty asked when Sisley closed the door to her room again.

"They are with Sam and Cate, our friends from Beach Cove," Sisley replied. "Pippa and Sam's granddaughter, Brooke, are BFFs. I'm sure they're having the best time. The older kids, I mean." She giggled guiltily. "I'm expecting a call from Sam about Lovie. She loves the older girls, though. Maybe she'll be all right."

Kitty inhaled a deep breath, tasting Pine-Sol and book dust on her tongue. "Sisley, I hate to ask a favor," she said haltingly, stopping in front of the huge window. The sun was warm.

Sisley folded her hands. "If you do, then you don't realize how many favors I've called in since coming to Bay Harbor," she said sincerely. "Go right ahead and ask. What can I do for you?"

"I'm wondering whether I could rent space here," Kitty said. The thought had come to her in Sisley's studio. There was a second door opposite it. If it looked anything like what Kitty had just seen, it would be perfect for making hats. Space and light, a couple of electrical outlets, and desks were all she needed. "I could do with a proper studio for making hats and taking on sewing projects. I've always worked from home, but you know..." She let the sentence trail off since Sisley did know the apartment was too small for any kind of home business.Her niece's eyes lit up. "Yes!" she said without hesitation and pointed at the second door Kitty was trying hard not to eye too longingly. "Let me show you the other room. I was going to use it to store paintings since we had no other plans. To be honest, I have plenty of space in my own studio, especially once I start to hang them for viewing out here."

Kitty moistened her lips. The next part was hard. "Only—I might not be able to pay very much rent right away." She glanced at her feet. "I lost most of my savings selling my bungalow in Seal Harbor.

It wasn't up to a code that was made for wealthy people. Or maybe it was made to get people like me out. Either way, I have to start from scratch."

"Oh Kitty." Sisley's hand lightly touched her arm. "None of us can pay for this space; we took a gamble talking to Mr. Brennan, and it paid off. Like I said, we got it for a song and a promise. Let me talk with Morris. I'm sure he won't mind letting you use an empty room. Well, a little more than that. But it'll be no problem once your hats start selling again."

Unable to speak, Kitty nodded.

"Here." Sisley walked past her toward the second room, waving her to come. "Have a look. You'll like it."

Chapter 10

Sunny primly cleared her throat and squinted into the afternoon sun at Mela. "I decided to take the pie competition off Valerie's hands." She plucked a stalk of the wild grass that was shooting up everywhere on the field, turning it a sweet-smelling, swaying green.

"Are you sure?" Mela pulled her hand through the nodding grass. In late summer, the grass would turn bright gold. But now, in June, it was still green, and the stalks smelled of rain when you broke them. As if her years with a bad hip had made her impatient to always be moving now, Sunny's capable hands bent the long stalk, wrapping and unwrapping it into pretzel shapes. She didn't seem to notice, looking at her niece.

Mela handed Sunny the smoker and pulled off her beekeeping hat with the veil of black netting and shook out her hair. The bees were doing well, and she'd had to swap the full honeycombs for empty ones earlier than expected. It was always warm under the tightly woven straw, and she needed to wipe the sweat from her brow and forehead.

"Are you sure?" She handed Sunny the hat too and lifted the heavy nuke box, then started walking toward the barn where they kept the bee things.

On the terrace by the house, Amelie, Sam, and Cate were drinking coffee and eating lemon pie. Even with the warm scents of honey and beeswax in the air, Mela detected the delicious smells of Sunny and Amelie's latest bake-off. She smiled at the kids, who were playing a game that involved Pippa and Brooke jumping down the low wall in silly ways. Lovie and the twins who belonged to Tom and Em, the owners of the Beach Cove Café and Bakery, were rolling with laughter on a thick quilt spread on the ground.

"It's a pie contest. How can I not do it?" Sunny walked with her, easily stepping around the thorny heaps of wild roses and bushels of tiger lilies sprouting in the grass. "Besides, Valerie needs a break. Maybe she'll be less tense when she has a little room to breathe."

Mela glanced at her aunt and had to press her lips together to keep from smiling at the determined look in Sunny's eyes. "Good for you. But it's going to be a lot."

"I have time. Now that Alice Harper is watching the kids every chance she gets, I'll have to find something else to do."

"It sure will be better for my waist," Mela joked. "It's true that you like pies. If you're not going to judge them, you'll probably spend all your time baking them." And then, Mela would eat them, no matter whether she meant to stay away from the guilty calories or not. She winked at her aunt.

"I don't make you eat anything," Sunny said, looking satisfied with herself. "It's your own fault if you're getting fat."

Mela chuckled. She was a far way from fat, but she wasn't as trim as she used to be before Sunny took over the cooking and baking. "I guess you're right. You look great, by the way."

"Oh. Thank you. You do too. I was joking." Sunny grinned impishly. "Mostly."

When they met, Sunny had been bound to her small room at the Beach Motel. Unable to walk, she'd been heavy, pale, and more than a little dejected at the thought of aging out of an active life.

But now that she'd found family and braved knee-replacement surgery, she was no longer overweight, and her eyes sparkled, and she was outside enough to have a light tan even in the winter. It was easy to see that Sunny was happy. Living in Seasweet Lane was good for her, and she loved being surrounded by a family growing all the time as babies and long-lost relatives joined them.

"Compliments aside, I sat down with Valerie to talk it through." Sunny sidestepped a patch of milkweed. "It took a surprisingly long time. I don't mind saying that."

"You hashed everything out? You know what to do?" They'd reached the sandy path leading to the barn and stepped out of the field.

Sunny patted the burrs off her pants. "Of course I know what to do, Mela. It's a pie contest. I'm old, not stupid."

"It can't be as easy as simply judging the pies?"

"Mostly. But because there are so many entries, there are several elimination rounds, like in a game show."

"I figured Valerie would have a lot of rules to judge them...more perfectly," Mela said. "I'm just teasing, Sunny. Valerie's quite nice if you can get past the prickles."

"I know what you mean." Sunny was well aware of Valerie's despotic way of running the market. "But I agree. She's coming along. I think she allowed two sincere opinions to slip through the mask while we talked. To tell the truth, they were pretty much the only ones I agreed with."

Mela pushed the barn door open. "We can work with two. That's a good beginning."

"I also told her two of my own opinions," Sunny shared. "I have to hand it to her; she rallies when she has to."

"Let's ask her over for brunch this weekend." Mela set down the nuke, then took the veil and hat from her aunt and hung them up. Often, she didn't need to wear a veil, but the bees were restless after the long spring rains and more eager than usual to defend their sweet treasure.

Sunny opened the smoker and scraped the last of the smoldering burlap on the ground. The smoke calmed the bees, and even to Mela it smelled comforting, but Sunny didn't like the scent.

She stepped on the burlap until it stopped smoking and wrinkled her nose. "Smells like the barn is burning. And you smell like a firefighter."

"I feel like one too." Mela pulled her aunt's arm through her own and marched her back in the sweet sea air. "We'll leave the door open, so it airs out."

"I've already run into a snag," Sunny confided as they joined Amelie and their guests from Beach Cove at the patio table and started to talk about the contest.

Amelie leaned forward. "What is it? I always said the competition was rigged!"

Cate pulled a face as if she agreed. "I've submitted my poppy cake for years now and always get fourteenth place. *Fourteenth*. My daughter has a bakery selling this very cake, and it's sold out by ten a.m. There's no way it's not at least a five."

"Well, now that Sunny's running it, we'll see whether that's true," Sam groaned. "Once your poppy cake finds justice, maybe you won't have to mention it all the time anymore."

"I don't mention it all the time," Cate said mildly and sipped her tea. "Only once or twice a year. You and I have just spent a lot of years together. You can always stop hanging out if I bore you."

"I might," Sam said dryly. "Hand me the lemon cake, will you?" She nodded at the three-tier lemon cake with layers of fluffy white sponge cake, tart lemon curd, and sweet cream cheese frosting.

Mela chuckled, but Amelie rose to push slices on Sam's, Mela's, and Sunny's plates, wiping a drip of glaze from the tablecloth with her finger. "Don't let them get you off topic, Sunny. I want to know everything. What snag did you run into with the pie contest?"

"Actually, there are two." Sunny eyed the luscious calorie bomb on her plate. Like Mela's, her diet plans weren't immune to delicious scents and sights. With a small sigh, she picked up her fork and pushed a piece of the spongy slice on it. "One, there are over four hundred entries this year. The deadline isn't even until two weeks from now."

Amelie's eyes widened. "Wow. That's...a lot."

"Told you," Sam murmured to Cate, who pointed at the cake to indicate Sam would do better eating than commenting.

Sunny balanced her bite in the air. "I can't tell you how many people said they bake for relaxation. I guess I'm not the only one."

"Baking is very therapeutic," Amelie confirmed. "I recommend making bread to my clients. It's a great way to take your mind off your worries. I do it too."

"Ah, you do it when you're relaxed. It's in your genes." Sunny tasted the lemon pie and cleaned her palate with a sip of coffee.

Mela poured herself a glass of lemonade from the pitcher. The kids had tuckered themselves out and were crawling on all fours around the table, giggling. Even Lovie could play that game.

"We're caterpillars!" Pippa, the eldest, called out when she noticed Mela. "Look! Sam! *Sam*! Watch me!" She lay on her belly and pushed her arms flat against her side, wiggling like an inchworm. Behind her, Cate's grandchildren, the twins, squeaked with laughter. Brooke, while holding her place in line, had flipped over and lay on her back like a sun worshipper, pale arms and golden hair spread wide, her head turned and her eyes fixed on the rolling sea behind the field. Lovie had plunked down by her feet, studying the handful of purple lavender sprigs she'd ripped out.

"Great! You're very...caterpillary."

Amelie rose to pick up Lovie, smelling the lavender the baby thrust at her as she returned. "All right, four hundred contestants. What's the other snag?"

Sunny's lids dropped to veil her eyes, and her voice softened. Everyone leaned forward to hear. "Connie Becowitz dropped by the house yesterday."

"Who's Connie Becowitz?" Mela asked. "I've never heard that name in my life."

"Exactly." Sunny's eyes closed another fraction. "Me neither. She lives in Bay Port."

"Bay Port? What did she want?" Sam asked, sounding suspicious.

"She wanted to tell me that her recipe was carried over here on the *Mayflower*." Sunny leaned back. "She thought it'd be best if I *knew* so I could take the recipe's history into consideration. She claimed Valerie always thought it was very interesting where recipes came from."

Amelie pulled her chin into her throat. "The Mayflower?"

"Yes," Sunny confirmed. "Guess what I did?"

Mela felt her eyes widen. "Oh no. What did you do?"

"I looked up the recipe. It's from allcooks.com." Sunny exhaled heavily. "And it wasn't even her who posted it—unless she's masquerading as an Indian guy in his twenties. What am I supposed to do with that?"

Everyone sank back into their comfortable, crackling wicker chairs. "Aha!" Cate said in a tone of deep conviction. "Hence the fourteenth place. *I* never go around claiming it came from the Mayflower."

"Write her an email and ask," Sam said. She was always very practical-minded. "My feeling is she'll not enter this year. She'll pretend she's offended but let her save face."

"I can try," Sunny said. "Oh. Hey! What are you lot doing?"

The kids had crawled under the table and were clamoring for the gummy bears Mela had put out for them. For a while, the women were busy negotiating how many more gummies each could have.

The porch door opened behind Mela. "And what are you ladies up to today?" a deep voice asked.

Chapter 11

Mela looked up. "Peter! Charlie! You managed to get away."

"Travis is manning the front desk for now." Peter came to kiss her while Charlie did the same for Amelie and tickled Lovie, who squealed happily.

The wide wicker chairs were taken, so Peter pulled two folding chairs from the barn and brought them over. The brothers joined them at the table, eagerly accepting large slices of cake.

"This is delicious," Peter announced, his cheeks full of lemon curd and cream cheese frosting. "Hey Sunny, you never baked a cake like this for me."

"You didn't have a kitchen worth baking in," Sunny shot back.

Peter winked at her and shoveled another decadent bite into his mouth. After Sunny lost her home and worldly possessions to a landslide, he'd taken her in. It hadn't been an easy arrangement for either of them, but the two fought their way through the tough times together. Peter was like a son to Sunny now, and while he pretended to treat her like a pesky mother-in-law, Peter adored Sunny and would do anything for her.

"This is the best I've ever tasted," Charlie declared.

"You spend too much time with your cowboys in the outback." Despite the protest, Sunny's cheeks warmed with pleasure.

"Not all my time." Charlie put his empty plate back on the table. "Sunny, we meant to ask you something."

The kids, clutching handfuls of gummy bears despite the negotiations, made their getaway into a hollowed-out lilac bush.

Giggling with glee, the babies crawled as fast as they could to follow Brooke and Pippa.

Peter had already finished as well. "Your cakes taste unbelievable, Sunny. We could use your baking at the motel. Our guests have a tough time finding enough places to eat." He smiled at Sam and Cate. "Ellie and Maisie sent the first guests, thanks to you. The phone's been ringing off the hook since then."

Sam and Cate exchanged a glance. "Do you have any British tourists?" Cate asked. "Or fake-British, all of them more or less giving off the same vibe?"

"A lot of them, actually." Peter cocked his head. "How do you know? Did Mela mention it?"

"No. But that's the sort usually coming to stay at the Beach Cove Inn. Hmm." Cate squinted as if trying to put together the pieces of a puzzle.

"Cate. It's fine," Sam said softly. "We promised."

Mela would have liked to know what was going on in Beach Cove. Maybe, someday when she had time to spare, she'd visit Maisie at the Beach Cove Inn to find out.

Peter looked from Sam to Cate and back, then he continued. "Anyways, Sunny, my brother and I were wondering about offering our guests more than rooms. Cake, in particular. And breakfast too."

"What do you mean?" Sunny asked. "Do you want me to deliver cake and bread?"

Charlie cleared his throat. "Bay Harbor needs more infrastructure. I'm determined to bring this town back to life; it's too beautiful to go broke. The motel brings in tourists, but that's only the beginning. We need more stores and restaurants. We need a *bakery*. We need music and books and arts. The kids are taking care of that, and the stores and restaurants are coming, but..." He reached out.

Sunny narrowed her eyes but gave him her hand.

"We would like you to run a bakery," Charlie said. "That caters to both the town and the Beach Motel. I want your pies to make a difference."

"Charlie and I only just talked it over this morning," Peter added, coming to his brother's aid. "We'd tossed ideas around before, but we weren't sure we could pull it off." He tapped the rim of his cake plate. "There's been a development, a space we could buy for a bakery. All we need are bakers."

"Be serious, Peter." Sunny drew her hand back. "Are you serious, or are you joking?"

"Serious," he reassured Sunny. "Very serious. We *need* better bread in this town. We need more places where people can come together and enjoy themselves."

"A bakery does wonders for the community," Cate agreed. "My daughter can confirm how busy she is running the one in Beach Cove. She'd be delighted to help you get off to a good start."

"Oh." Sunny blinked. "You really are serious."

"Amelie?" Charlie turned to his high school sweetheart and mother of his son. He'd loved her all his life, and it showed on his face whenever he looked at her.

"Yes." Amelie sat up straighter. "Sunny, Charlie and I sort of, hypothetically, talked about it before. I don't have so many clients anymore since... Well, since Michael, the guy who manages the Bay Harbor bank, has taken up against me. I could go in half-time with you."

"Ehr-hmm." Sunny cleared her throat. "Are you all talking about me running a proper *bakery*?" She still looked like she couldn't believe what she was hearing.

"Yes!" they replied in chorus.

Mela put a hand on her aunt's arm. "Whatever they want, though, you do what's best for you," she said. "Personally, I think you should leave plenty of time for beach walks and playing with the kids."

"We don't mean to put Sunny to hard labor," Charlie cut in. "I'll run the business side of things, obviously, and we'll train people to help. But we want Sunny to be the head of the operation. She knows how to bake and has fantastic recipes. She'll be the best at training new bakers." He nodded at the tiered lemon torte. "I promise a slice of this will make an impression on our vacationers. They'll never forget the day they stopped by at Sunny's. And our townspeople deserve to have the best we can offer."

"Yes." Sunny stood, her eyes on Amelie. "Amelie, you and me? We'll go into business together?"

Amelie stood too. Mela stilled, seeing the joy on her friend's face. Amelie's father gambled away the family's famous bakery chain, and the loss had always weighed on her.

"You and me, Sunny." Amelie held out a hand, and Sunny shook over the lemon curd.

"It has a dash of rosewater in it," Sunny whispered. "That's the secret."

Amelie's eyes widened. "Oh, of course. I should have known."

Charlie and Peter stood too, beaming. "The Beach Motel will be your first and best customer," Charlie promised. "We'll give you good terms. You'll be surprised at how much a bakery can make."

Mela shook her head. She was sure the deal would be good—Charlie would do anything to make Amelie happy, and Peter would always look after Sunny.

She turned to him. "Peter, I'm worried it'll be too much for Sunny."

"Fiddlesticks," Sunny declared briskly, having caught the words. "I've wanted a bakery. I'll sleep when I'm dead!"

"You never once said you wanted a bakery," Mela pointed out. "And may I remind you that you'd have to get up before dawn to bake if you commit to catering breakfast rolls?"

"I'll do what I want." A stubborn look clouded Sunny's eyes.

"You'll sleep while it's dark outside," Peter told his aunt-in-law firmly. "Charlie, here we go. She's not going to listen."

Everyone laughed at the exasperation in his voice.

"We'll hire people," Charlie said again. "We'll make it work."

"Sit down, everyone." Mela rose. "I'm going to make a fresh pot of tea, and then we will talk about details. I'm not going to let Sunny stumble into something half-cooked."

"I don't need your permission," Sunny grumbled. "I can open a bakery if I want, and I want."

"Exactly." Charlie crossed his hands over his lean stomach. "Mela, I promise it'll be Sunny's dream job. I have a stack of names of locals eager for a job in town, and Amelie's already picked out the ones who can bake. Sunny can pick the ones she likes."

"Uh. Yes. There are a few nice women you'll want on the team, Sunny," Amelie said.

"Maybe Em should hire a few people too," Cate mused. "It's time she and Tom work less and get to play more with the kids. They have the money to make it happen."

Sunny inhaled. "Great bakers, jobs, community...all joking aside, I really think we have something."

Chapter 12

Mela shook her head. "I suppose Sunny already works from morning to night anyway... I'm not going to keep you from doing what you like and helping the town, dear aunt. I'll get the tea and the upside-down orange cake you made. But then we *will* talk about the details. I have only one aunt, and I wish to keep her as happy and healthy as I can."

She left, striding past the others into the house. Already, Charlie was laying out a plan for how to make it work, but Peter followed her, pulling her into his arms.

"It'll be great," he murmured into her hair. "Charlie has the money to do it in style. Nobody has to work themselves to the bone, least of all Sunny and Amelie. They'll only do as much as they like. We set it up that way on purpose."

Mela smiled up at him. "You want the best for Sunny."

"Of course I do. I shouldn't have sprung this at you. You're used to having Sunny at home. Are you all right?"

"As long as Sunny can stop working whenever she wants."

"That's a promise." He squinted at her. "What's on your mind lately? You seem a bit worried."

Mela sighed. "I am. Not about Sunny but about Kitty," she admitted. "She's miserable. She's had to take care of herself all her life, but I think this time, she could really use help."

"We're here to help. But there's nothing we can do until she wants our help."

"Everyone's so happy. The kids all found partners and are starting families and new careers. Everyone's blossoming. Only Kitty seems to get more depressed by the day. She was so cheerful when I first met her, but now she's back on her heels, and I can tell she feels like a stranger in Bay Harbor. I wish she would trust me. I wish she were used to people having her back."

"You lost your mother young, but Julie loved you. Her mother clearly didn't want children. Even if she did her best...it'd be a miracle if Kitty didn't have some trust issues."

"I know. Well, at least she asked Sisley about the upstairs space in the library. Of course the kids are happy to let her use it. Maybe that will help bring us together."

"That's good. I'm glad she asked." Peter let Mela go and leaned against the counter. After a while, he cleared his throat. "Talking about space... We bought the old mill for the bakery."

Mela's eyes widened. "The old mill by the cranberry bog?"

"It's got a view of the sea. Sunny will love it."

"It's a mill. It has wooden wings. It makes flour. Or used to, in the olden days."

"Charlie already hired a team to gut it. He's going all in."

Mela grabbed the kettle and filled it at the sink. "How much money does Charlie *have*?" she asked weakly.

"Millions," Peter said confidently. "Possibly more. I can tell you Charlie bought Amelie the new house like other men buy their girlfriends a box of chocolate."

"What do you mean *more*? He's a billionaire?"

Peter shrugged. "At this point, I wouldn't be surprised. He dropped hints that he invested big in bitcoin and sold when it was at its highest. The good thing is he's determined to put his hometown back on her feet. Already, the motel is attracting more tourists than Bay Harbor can handle."

Mela flicked on the stove and set the kettle on the biggest flame. She used to make a big salary and had had money for most of her adult life. Even after the divorce, she still had enough to comfortably take care of her family and help her friends. But Charlie was operating on a different level.

"I'm happy your brother found his way back home." She rinsed the teapot and sprinkled tea leaves into the diffuser egg. "Bay Harbor is going to be just fine with the two of you on the job."

"Bay Harbor will be just fine," Peter confirmed. "Mela, there's one other thing I was going to tell you… The previous owner lived in the mill before she passed away. The mill needs work, but the apartment in the back is beautiful. We're leaving it as is, with the exception of a few touch-ups in the bathroom and the kitchen."

"And?" Mela glanced at him as she pulled the orange upside-down cake out of the fridge. Baked in a cast-iron skillet, it had a bright orange base, a crunchy almond crust, and was topped with a sweet brown sugar glaze. Even cold, the caramelized oranges smelled delicious. Mela set it down. "Are you thinking about moving out of the motel, Peter?"

"I'm thinking about you and me," he said gently. "I'm not asking you to get married because I realize you like things the way they are. But…"

Mela dried her hands on a towel. "But you…what?"

"I don't need a marriage certificate, either, but I would like to live together," Peter admitted. "I've barely seen you in the last few weeks because we've both been busy. But I want to fall asleep each night with my arms around you. I want to live with you and know that we're doing this together."

"This…what?" She smiled up at him.

"This everything." He smiled back. "I can't take my eyes off you. I can't stop thinking about you. And I can't believe how lucky I am to be with you."

"Aww." Mela put the towel down and came to him. "Tell me more."

"Your eyes sparkle like the sea in the moonlight. And I love the way you light up the room when you walk in. Every day, you look more beautiful than the day before."

"Very nice. I love you too." She rose on tiptoes to kiss him.

He kissed her back. The kiss started off tender and gentle, full of warmth and affection, but soon Peter's lingering lips sent sparks of electricity through Mela. She broke away. It was hardly the time...though she would have liked to make time. It was true that they had not seen enough of each other. She missed him too.

Peter cleared his throat. "I know how much your independence means to you. I don't want to take it from you. But I would like more."

"I would like more too."

Peter's expression changed as if he could hardly believe his ears. He pulled her closer and hugged her tightly to him. "You have no idea how I've wanted to hear you say that."

A wave of joy surged through her. Her marriage had lacked passion, but with Peter, it was different. Mela laid her head on his chest, listening to her childhood hero's steady heartbeat. Then she remembered what they'd been talking about. "What do you and I have to do with the apartment in the mill?" Mela asked. "I can't move out of this house. It means too much to me."

"Nor would I ask that of you." Peter loosened his grip, and Mela, after giving him one more quick kiss, returned to the task of making tea and plating the cake. "It's more of a heads-up."

"For?"

He cleared his throat. "I fully expect Sunny to fall in love with the mill the moment she sees it. I'd never suggest she move out, but I need you to brace yourself—she'll want to live in the mill. She likes her independence just as much as you do."

"Oh." Now that he said it, Mela knew it would make sense for her aunt. Sunny's bedroom upstairs was small, and if one day she wouldn't be able to climb the stairs, there was only a converted pantry off the kitchen.

"I suppose if she brings it up herself…" She pressed her lips together. She'd found her aunt late and loved living together. But it could be difficult too. There was only a small bathroom in the old house, and sound traveled much too easily through the thin walls of the bedrooms. When Peter stayed over, pillow talk—or any other sound—was out of the question. And Sunny, on her side, didn't love the narrow staircase or the fact that she had to share her kitchen with her niece. "I mean, I see your point. I'm not going to say anything, though, and you and your brother should not do it, either. Sunny has to fall in love with the apartment and bring up moving herself."

"I agree." Peter nodded. "And I'm sure she will. You'll understand when you see it. It really is beautiful. It'll be even better once Charlie's through with it." He took a breath. "But I just wanted you to know how much I love you and that I want this to happen. I want to live with you. In the same house."

Mela smiled up at him. She still had times when she couldn't believe she'd found Peter again. She loved him as a child, and she'd loved him ever since. He was the man she measured all the other men in her life against, even if she hadn't realized it. Their second chance came about only by accident. She'd missed many years with Peter while she was married to the wrong man. But the present was perfect. It was enough.

"I want to live with you too," she said simply.

As they held each other close, Mela knew they would take this step in their relationship. Everything would turn out well, whether or not Sunny decided to stay. Because together, they could do anything.

Chapter 13

Kitty pressed the number on her screen. Clutching her phone, she walked to the window of her new studio overlooking the rooftops of Bay Harbor. Mid-morning light flooded in warm and golden, gleaming on her work desk and the beautiful shelves salvaged from the reading hall. The small handful of hats she had made barely started to fill one of them.

"Kitty? It's been a while." The voice was familiar yet deeper than she remembered.

"Hi, Clyde? How are you?" Clyde Carsten. The boy who sat next to Kitty in science and English during freshman year in high school. Not Kitty's choice; their teachers seated them. Almost every day, Clyde asked her out even though Kitty only shook her head and ignored him. Then he started to bring her flowers and bonbons and write her little notes. Kitty found them back at home in her book bag, and she tore them up and tossed them. But he wore her down by lavishing attention on her when nobody else did. In the end, she agreed to a date, too flattered to follow her gut instinct and too naive to understand the hints some of the girls dropped.

There was only one date. In the dark back seats at a movie theater. It ended prematurely with a lunge and a sprint.

Clyde lunged to grab her, and Kitty sprinted away from him.

It hadn't been that easy to get free. He'd pinned her good, his mouth groping for hers and his body pressing into her. But she managed to wiggle out from under him by kicking up her knee in his crotch. She ran out, past the other movie goers who looked but didn't say anything.

Shaking, she started walking home from the movie theater. For five miles in the dark, she steamed over Clyde pinning her against the seat, disgusted with the feel of his body that had burned its impression on her skin. Every now and then that night she ran, her legs powered by anger. And fear, because Kitty didn't like the dark and she was afraid Clyde would come after her, looking to finish what he'd started. Even though they lived in Portland, not all streets had lamp posts and not all building doorways lights to see who stood there.

The next day, Clyde pretended nothing had happened when they dissected a grasshopper in biology class. Not only was he not sorry for grabbing her or worried whether she'd made it home safely, he assumed they would go out again. When Kitty told him what she thought of his behavior, he sneered, tossed his forceps into the dissection tray, and stormed out of the class. As if she'd done him an injustice. The teacher even docked Kitty points because alone, she couldn't finish the project before class ended.

For the rest of the semester, they ignored each other. But soon, wild rumors about Kitty spread like wildfire through the school. It didn't take much brainpower to put two and two together and figure out who started them.

Kitty asked for new seats, kept her head down and her grades up. But she never forgot Clyde.

When she looked up the name of the fashion purchaser at Pipers, the biggest department store in Bay Port, and found it was him, her hands had balled into fists. Hard enough for her fingernails to dig into her skin.

But Kitty needed a game changer, something solid that would carry her and put money back into her account. A department store ordering on a regular basis could be the break she was looking for. The lunge in the movie theater had been a long time ago, and times had changed. Surely life had taught Clyde better by now.

"I'm very well, thanks for asking. How are you yourself, Kitty?"

"I'm all right."

"I lost track of you. Most people from high school, actually." He laughed, sounding pleased with this. His voice was deeper than it used to be, and he was friendly enough, taking her call like this. "I can't remember much of what happened back then. It's so long ago. Maybe I prefer to forget too. I was a handful, wasn't I?"

Skipping the answer, Kitty came straight to her point. "I'm a hat maker," she said before she could lose her nerve. "I was looking up department stores that might carry hats and was surprised to see your name."

"I'm surprised too." He laughed. "Couldn't tell you how it happened."

"I didn't think you were interested in fashion, of all things."

"Live and learn, Kitty. Live and learn. I include myself in that. I didn't see it coming either." He chuckled comfortably.

Maybe life really had pulled and pushed him into the shape of a decent person. "Listen, does Piper carry hats?" Kitty asked. The words came too quickly.

There was a short pause. "Nothing special as far as I remember," he said then. "Cheap one-size-fits-all fedoras for fashionable teens. Honestly, that's all I can think of off the top of my hat. Uh—head." He laughed. "In the winter we offer the usual selection of knit hats of course, but it's all mass-produced by big names. Kors, Klein, that sort of thing. If you're a milliner, you probably have something else in mind?"

"I make a wide variety of hats," she said bravely. "I mostly sell them online, and I have very good references from my customers. I was hoping Pipers would be interested in carrying them. I live in Bay Harbor now, so it'd be local to the area. I'm sure buying local is a selling point as well as PR for Pipers."

Kitty didn't like advertising herself, and she had never pitched to a store. She didn't know if she was doing it right. Despite the warm light and the inviting space around her, she felt like she was standing in a freezer and a hundred tiny pins were pricking her skin. She shook out her hand to get the blood flowing again.

"I agree." Clyde hummed a tuneless melody, and Kitty heard him leaf through paper. "Well, if you're local, why don't we set up a meeting? Show me what you've got."

An electric current flashed through Kitty, constricting her lungs. Were those the words he'd said while lunging at her? She shook her head. No. It was nerves. Her nerves were playing tricks on her. She'd never remembered Clyde saying those words before. Only his pupils, which were pinpricks in the flickering light from the movie.

She inhaled, forcing her airway open. "When's a good time?"

"The sooner, the better." More leafing of paper. "I'm here until five. Then I go home to the old ball and chain." He laughed again. "Just kidding. She's the love of my life. Happily married for two decades. Two adorable sons too, though they're in college."

"Oh. Congratulations." Kitty checked the time on the oversized London station clock she'd hung on the wall. She bought it with the money from her first hat sale in a Seal Harbor antiquity store. Whether or not it really was from London, she loved the clock. "I can be there before five. Where do I find you?"

"Ask any Pipers girl for the secret elevator." Again he laughed as if it was a joke. "I'm upstairs."

Kitty frowned. "Pipers girl as in...sales associate?"

"Of course. Listen, I gotta go, big meeting coming up. I'm looking forward to seeing you, Kitty. My schedule's pretty tight, so we won't have another chance for a while. Don't leave me hanging, okay?"

"I'll be there. Thanks for the opportunity." Kitty hung up and stared at her phone. Maybe life had pushed and pulled the boy she knew into a decent person. Maybe it was just her mind playing tricks. And maybe, Clyde was still the same as he'd been back in school.

"Not much time," she whispered to call herself to order. Her schoolgirl musings wouldn't dig her out of the hole she was in. "Now, what to take?"

Pickings were slim. Kitty made hats to custom order; she did not mass-produce them. Once a creation was finished, she shipped it off in one of the cute hat boxes saying *Kitty's Custom Crowns*. She always included a personal note and a gift of a pink rhinestone pin to fix to the hatband, but of course she didn't need to do that for Clyde. Either way, there were few hats on the shelf.

Kitty pulled a handful of hat boxes in assorted sizes from the top shelf. She'd stacked them just yesterday but now pried open the lids and lined them with purple tissue paper. To show off her range, she picked a feathered fascinator, a majestic wide brim she'd started for the Ascot order before it fell through, and a jaunty unisex trilby meant for teens going on beach walks in the summer. She nestled them into the paper and carefully closed the boxes.

After short consideration, she also bagged a couple of her special berets and caps—silk lining to tame wavy hair and curls on frizzy days or absorbent cotton for drying freshly washed hair—and a selection of fabrics and decorative elements in case Clyde still needed to see more. Gripping her boxes and bags, she opened the studio door and kicked it shut behind her with a foot.

Downstairs was noise and shouting. Morris was overseeing the arrival of his grand piano. In a lucky coincidence, the old library's only structural damage happened to be some rotted siding next to the back door. A leaking gutter caused it. The builder had removed the siding and even some of the wall.

Morris was taking advantage of the gaping hole to bring in his bulky instrument. One leg had hooked into the wooden scaffolding of the remaining wall, causing a lot of groans from those carrying the weight of the thing as they shifted here and there to dislodge it. Morris and the captain of the movers were shouting at each other to navigate the tight spot with scratches to the shiny finish.

Kitty squeezed past a bulky fisherman in a navy sweater who was waving the movers into position with hands as big as lobster traps. "Excuse me," she mumbled, only earning herself a fierce glare.

"Hi, Kitty! Don't mind us. We'll get her in eventually!" Morris had spotted her and waved a greeting.

"Hey!" Hands too full to wave, Kitty nodded a greeting back and smiled. "Good luck over there."

"It has nothing to do with luck," the captain grumbled. "Hey! Watch it, Larsen. You're as bad at this as at filleting bass."

"As soon as I set this thing down, I'll fillet you outside," Larsen growled. His knees were buckling under the weight of the piano, but his spirit seemed unbroken.

The shouting and banging hadn't gone unnoticed by the small town. Already, people were knocking on the door and asking when the first concert would happen, whether they could rent the place for wedding receptions and sweet sixteens, and if it was true there would be a gallery upstairs. Could they showcase their own aquarelles maybe?

Even now, Johanna stood in a corner with a group of curious locals who were gathering to watch the interesting spectacle. When she saw Kitty, she came to meet her, lithely dodging movers and boxes and waving hands as she crossed the hall.

Johanna was in charge of the library's books that had been part of the bargain. A lot of them would be donated, some they would keep. Sam Bowers had offered to buy the bulk of what was left. She had a store for antique books in Beach Cove and spent hours sifting through the books on the shelves digging for treasure.

Sometimes she had help from a tall man with stooped shoulders and heavily lidded eyes. His name was Vince. Vince was always impeccably polite, but Kitty felt the ground under her feet turn spongy every time he looked at her. Maybe it was her knees. Why the man affected her so, she couldn't tell. It was just one of the many mysteries about Beach Cove and its inhabitants.

Johanna had reached her. "Hi. I needed an excuse to get away. I've been fielding questions since this morning." She smiled. "Do you need help with the boxes?"

"Hi, Johanna. Thanks, but I got it." Kitty smiled and lifted her hands to show that the bulky boxes were easy to carry.

"Oh come on, let me have one." Johanna glanced over her shoulder. "Mrs. Tenner will get me otherwise, and I really have no idea whether she can have a treasure hunt race through the old library's stacks for her eight-year-old. There must be some insurance liability for books toppling on nosy kids."

Kitty chuckled and handed Johanna a box and a bag. She too had wielded some of Mrs. Tenner's questions about knitting competitions and birthday parties.

"Where are we taking them? I thought the farmers market was only on weekends?" Johanna pushed back her hair.

She was very pretty, and a trilby would draw attention to her bright features. Kitty couldn't help but mentally measure the young woman's head. Johanna would be a great hat model. "I have a meeting with the fashion purchaser at Pipers. I'm on my way over there."

"Wow." Johanna seemed impressed. "Do they carry hats?"

Kitty blew out a breath as Clyde's voice came back to her. "He said he couldn't remember, other than winter hats and a fedora here and there," she admitted. "Which is more of a no than a yes. The hope is I will change their mind."

"Are you going somewhere?" Walking backward toward them and keeping his eyes on his precious instrument, Morris was joining them.

"Yeah." Kitty had done things alone so long it seemed strange to get so much attention. "I have a meeting with the fashion purchaser at Pipers."

"Alone?" Morris tore his attention away from the movers. "Do you know the person you're meeting?"

"Sort of." Kitty was starting to feel uncomfortable. She wasn't used to being quizzed.

As if Johanna picked up on it, she smiled sweetly. "Kitty's older than you, Morris. She can handle herself."

"But thank you for your concern," Kitty added quickly. She liked her nephew and didn't want to be brusque.

"Only I've heard someone at the motel say something about Pipers... I can't remember what it was. But it left a bad taste in my mouth."

"Kitty, let me come." Johanna dusted her free hands on her jeans. "I need a couple of shirts anyway, and I don't like online shopping. I can have a look around the store while you're in your meeting. We can drive together."

Kitty tilted her head. "Thanks, Jo, but no babysitting needed. I still have a few years left in me."

"It's got nothing to do with babysitting. I promise I need the trip more than you do," Johanna declared. Without further ado, she hooked an arm under Kitty's and started walking. "We can take my car. I bought an adorable Mini last month, and I never get to drive it anywhere."

"In fact, Kitty, if *you* could watch *Jo* and make sure she's okay." The piano had been set in its designated space, and Morris was keeping pace with them. "I mean it. She tends to go on adventures when she's bored. She spent a whole night in Sunny's old house which sits on top of a landslide waiting to happen. She was in the basement, packing Sunny's belongings and hoping it wouldn't make the house drop into the sea—with her in it." The haunted look in his eyes told Kitty he wasn't just teasing.

"I don't need anyone looking out for me either," Johanna said archly. "Get that in your head, Morris Bryer Beckett."

Kitty knew just the color for the headband of Johanna's trilby—a raspberry red that would make her hair shine as much as her eyes. "All right," she relented. "Let's go together, Johanna. I need a new T-shirt myself."

"Maybe we'll make it a girls night and have dinner!" Johanna gave Morris a quick goodbye kiss on the cheek and waved at the piano crew.

"And maybe I'll have a boys night out with Peter and Charlie," Morris said. "Call me when you're back."

"Bye." Kitty leaned on the heavy front door with her shoulder. It creaked open, and they stepped into the heat of a beautiful coastal June day. The light chop of the waves slapping against the shore wall greeted them, bringing with it the soft cries of seabirds and the deep thrum of boats leaving port.

"I'll never get used to this." Johanna stretched out her arms as if she were trying to embrace the view before she laughed at herself. "Tagging after Mela and moving here was the best decision I ever made."

Kitty blinked in the sun. "I know," she said. It was clear that the young women Mela had brought with her—Sisley, Kimmie, and Johanna—were thriving and happy. Even Kitty had had an epiphany that Bay Harbor would be her home. Maybe its magic worked for old women too.

"I went through a rough spot because of family stuff, but now...every morning I wake up and the first thing I think is this can't be real. It's too good."

"I'm sure you deserve it." Kitty smiled at the wonder in Johanna's voice.

Waking up next to Morris probably had something to do with her happiness. In all her fifty-five years, Kitty had never been deeply in love herself, nor did she miss a man in her life. She was happy by herself—as long as her life wasn't falling in shambles around her. But Kitty still recognized true love when it crossed her path.

It was impossible not to smile back at Johanna's youthful enthusiasm, so Kitty did. "Are you sure you want to take your car? Mine is close by too."

"Oh! Yes, please, if you don't mind. So far, I've driven about two miles in it, and I'm dying to take it on the highway. It's in the parking lot in the back. We can take the shortcut over here." Johanna gestured toward the side of the library; between the building and the neighbor's faded picket fence was a walkway overgrown with June roses and the nodding buds of hydrangeas about to burst.

"Let's go," Kitty said. "I want to catch the man before he leaves for the day."

Chapter 14

"There it is." Gripping the arm handle of her seat for dear life, Kitty squinted at the tall building that shimmered, white and square, in the afternoon sun. Pipers was small compared to national chain department stores, but Bay Port wasn't a huge city. Still, it was bigger than the surrounding towns, and most of the local kids went to Bay Port University after graduation—it was far enough for a sniff of independence but close enough to visit home on weekends to do laundry and stock up on parental casseroles and cakes.

"Parking spot!" Johanna exclaimed and swerved wildly into a minuscule space between two hulking SUVs.

Kitty's hand shook as much as her knees when she opened her door and climbed out. "Next time we're taking my car," she muttered, glad to feel firm ground under her feet. Morris had not been overprotective when he wanted someone to keep an eye on his girlfriend. Johanna needed an eye on her. And she liked speed.

"But first you have to drive back with me." Johanna giggled.

Kitty inhaled the air to brace herself, then pulled her boxes from the tight backseat. The Mini was cute, but Kitty was more of a slow-Ford-truck-with-a-generous-bed kind of woman. "Okay. I'm going in."

"The air is different here. Not as clean." Johanna locked the car doors and caught up with her.

Inside, Pipers tried its best to keep pace with the big chains. There were displays scattered everywhere, and sales associates were helping mostly female customers pick perfumes and sundresses.

"You all right?" Johanna was already scanning the racks.

"Of course. I'll text you when I'm done." Kitty exhaled. Johanna was right. The air didn't taste like salt and sea here. The mingled scents of the perfumes choked Kitty, and she cleared her throat.

Johanna threw her a sharp glance. "Are you nervous?"

"Maybe a little," Kitty admitted. "No, a lot. I feel like I have eels squirming in my stomach. I hate putting myself forward."

"Oh, me too. Listen, I have your back. I'll walk you to the door. We can both look for clothes later."

Kitty wiped her sweaty palms on her jeans and nodded gratefully. "Let's ask someone where to go." She walked up to a makeup counter. "Excuse me... I'm looking for the elevator."

The woman Kitty had addressed turned to her. She was in her thirties and looked professional in a neat blouse and carefully coiffed hair, but her fine eyebrows drew together as if she couldn't believe what she'd just heard.

"Would you mind telling me where the elevator is?" Kitty repeated, puzzled.

"What?"

Kitty showed her boxes. "I have a meeting with the fashion purchase manager." Maybe putting it in context would help the woman understand. "He said to ask for the elevator upstairs."

"You have a meeting with Clyde Carsten?"

"Yes." Kitty let the boxes sink again.

The frown gave place to a blank look. "He's joking about the elevator," she said without explaining what the joke was. "He's in the back. Uh..." She waved at another associate to take over the counter, then gestured to Kitty and Johanna to follow. "I'll show you."

"Why did he say to ask for the elevator?" Johanna whispered as they wound their way between clothes and towels. "If it was an inside joke, it wasn't a good one judging by the reaction."

"Who knows." Kitty was here to land a contract. A shared sense of humor was too much to ask in the bargain.

"The door over there." The associate pointed. "Third to the right; go in together." She nodded at the hat boxes and turned to leave, saying over her shoulder, "Good luck with those. I love hats. People should wear them more often."

Kitty and Johanna slunk down a narrow, low hallway with a cement floor, neon lights, and managerial notes on a long, otherwise barren pinboard. The blue metal doors were marked with signs.

"Right next to the bathrooms," Johanna noted. "Classy."

It wasn't the private elevator to a lofty upstairs Kitty had expected either, but what did she know about small department stores? She'd never even been inside Pipers.

They duly passed the bathrooms and knocked on the door that read 'office.'

There was no answer.

"Right." Kitty tried the handle, and the door opened. "Hello? Anybody in?"

She walked into a small empty room with a single chair with synthetic upholstery crammed in the corner. The only other items in the room were a camera in an upper corner, red light blinking, and another door.

"In here, Kitty! Just keep going," Clyde called out, his voice muffled.

"I'll wait out here," Johanna whispered and took the chair. "Good luck."

"Thank you," Kitty whispered back. Two steps carried her to the second door. It was heavier and harder to push, the draft rubber at the bottom scraping over the hard floor. But once she managed to open it, Clyde was sitting behind a desk facing the door.

"Hi. Clyde?" She entered, letting the door close with a dull thud behind her. The man looked different from the boy she'd known. He was handsome, in a suit and with full black hair. Funny. Kitty distinctly remembered him as sandy blond, but maybe her brain played a trick on her.

Clyde powered off his computer screen. "Kitty! How nice to see you." He stood and rounded the desk, holding out his hand. "You haven't changed at all. How old are you again?"

Kitty shook his hand. Despite the question, she could tell he was shocked at how she looked. His eyes told her he'd expected someone else, someone closer to the slim fifteen-year-old from high school.

The stupidity of his expectation instantly melted her nerves. Maybe ten or fifteen years back, his disappointment would have made her feel insecure or yearn for the succulent glow of lost youth. But maybe not. Kitty liked how she looked. Body image struggles had never made it into the ranks of her problems.

"I'm almost fifty-six now," she said cheerfully, giving herself another six months for good measure. "But you look good yourself," she added graciously.

"Thank you for saying that." He winked.

"It's been a long time, hasn't it?" Kitty looked away.

"It sure has." He gestured to the chair in front of his desk and went to sit down behind it himself. "What can I do for you? You want to sell your hats at Pipers?"

"Yes, I'm looking to expand my business. Can I show you what I have?"

"Please." He nodded for her to use the empty corner of his desk. "I'd love to see. We're always looking for unique fashion and accessories."

Suddenly, it was easy. Kitty set a box on her lap and lifted the lid, then took out the fascinator. It was one of her favorite pieces—an elegant shade of red with only a hint of veil and matching decorative feather arrangement. It was both over and understated enough to be worn casually, the sort of hat that made women pay the wearer a compliment instead of rolling their eyes.

"This model is a little bit older, but it was featured in a well-known TV series about beautiful women wearing beautiful fashion." She smiled at the memory and told Clyde the name and episode. He jotted them down. "I had great demand for it right after the airing, and I think it could be used to drum up interest again."

"Ah." He took the hat from her. "Beautiful is certainly the right word for it. I see this with a tucked button-down shirt and a modern cut of jeans. Heels, of course. Maybe a couple of different tints to match the hair color of the season."

"Yes. Exactly." Kitty looked up, surprised he'd caught on so quickly. "That's exactly what they did on TV. They had slightly different colors for different takes to match the clothes."

Clyde stood. "I think I saw the episode. It's my job to monitor trends, after all. Would you loan it to me for a minute? I would like to put it on one of the girls outside, see how it looks in action, if you will. I'll be careful."

Kitty tried not to react to his use of the word girl for the women working in the store. "Sure." She stood too, but he motioned for her to sit.

"If you don't mind—I'd like to do it on my lonesome so I don't hurt your feelings if, you know, it doesn't work for me." He smiled an apology.

"Oh." Kitty sat back down. "My feelings are not that fragile, but sure. I'll just wait here, then."

"Thank you." He winked and left, closing the door behind him.

Kitty leaned back.

It was quiet now that Clyde was gone. Only the ticking of the large clock on the wall could be heard.

Not a minute passed before Kitty felt uncomfortable. She didn't mind Clyde taking her favorite hat out of the room. It took her a moment to realize it was the room itself that made her itch to leave.

She stood and inhaled, holding her breath. Then she let it out, the hissing of escaping air the only sound other than the clicking clock. No birds, no clonking pipes, nothing.

"Ugh. Like being wrapped in cotton," she muttered, picked up her things, and went to the door. She'd wait outside with Johanna instead of in this padded cell.

It took her a moment to drag open the heavy door. When she looked up from the darn rubber strip at the bottom, she froze.

Johanna was sitting pressed in the corner, Clyde planted inches in front of her. His crotch was at Johanna's eye level, and she was desperately trying not to look at it. The red fascinator sat on her head, and Clyde was tugging on it, half his fingers buried in Johanna's hair.

"Clyde!" Kitty dropped her boxes and strode across the room. "What are you doing? Stop!"

He wheeled around, his hands guiltily twitching down to hide his crotch.

"Kitty!" The chair scraped as Johanna angled it to escape her corner. She whisked the hat off her hair and held it out.

Kitty took it and stepped in front of the young woman. "He cornered you?"

"Uh." Johanna shuffled nervously. Kitty couldn't remember ever seeing her nervous. Ever since they first met, Johanna had shown nerves of steel.

"Of course I didn't." Clyde was still covering his crotch.

"Jo?" Kitty asked quietly. "Are you okay?"

"He asked if I could try on the hat to help you out. I don't know—I just wanted to have your back," Johanna said quietly.

Kitty lowered her chin and turned to Clyde. "You knew she was out here because you have a camera. You trapped her in that corner, making her think she needed to help me." Cold anger propelled her words, the same anger that had pumped her legs a long time ago.

The corners of Clyde's lips dropped in a sneer Kitty had seen before. "I have no idea what you're on about. I told you I was going to put the hat on one of the girls."

Kitty pointed a finger at him. "They're women, not girls. I should have known better than to come; knowing what I know, I should have listened to my instincts. I didn't do it in high school, either. But it's clear you're still the same person you were back in school when you tried to date rape me."

"What?" breathed Johanna behind her.

Clyde only blinked, but it was enough to let Kitty know he remembered as well as she did. "Nonsense," he said. "You were frigid. Everybody knew you were a prude. Nothing ever happened to you, least of all coming from me."

"Only because I ran." Kitty put the fascinator back into its box and stood, grabbing her load. "And me being frigid was not the rumor you spread, was it? You know what, Clyde?"

Something touched Kitty's arm. Johanna had pulled out her phone and was filming the exchange, the camera firmly directed at the purchase manager.

"Don't take photos of me. It's illegal." He angled his body away from the lens and stared back at Kitty. "What? Do I know what?"

"I should have kicked up a stink years ago."

He snorted. "Like anyone would believe the wanna-be memories of a fat old woman. You're desperate for attention, aren't you? I did nothing. And I'll sue you for slander."

"Too bad fat old women aren't as easily intimidated as schoolgirls and employees. Go ahead and sue me. Meanwhile, I'll send an email to our old classmates," Kitty said. "Girls were dropping hints left, right, and center. I didn't know what they meant, but I remember names, and I perfectly remember the words they said. I *know* I wasn't the only one, Clyde."

Clyde's cheeks had flushed a dusky red. "Don't," he warned. "I'll make sure you'll never sell a single hat in Bay Port. I'll make sure you never sell a hat anywhere."

"As if I care about doing business with Pipers anymore." Kitty shook her head at how far off the man was. "Life hasn't taught you a lesson you need to learn. Maybe I can do it." She glanced at the door into the corridor, ready to get out.

It didn't have a handle on the inside.

Kitty felt her heartbeat speed up like an alarmed drummer hitting his sticks faster.

"Jo?" She reached to the back as if she needed to make sure Johanna was still safely behind her.

"I caught that on camera," Johanna whispered. "It's a threat."

"Open the door for us," Kitty said in a low voice. "Right now, Clyde."

"Put the phone away!" Clyde craned his neck to see Johanna. "Are you filming? You're not allowed to film in here!"

"Keep filming, Jo. Clyde, open the door," Kitty repeated. "Or all hell is going to break loose. That's a promise."

"I don't have to get out to post this footage on YouTube," Johanna said. "My brother-in-law is a cop, and so is one of my best friends. They get notifications the second I post, and you can bet they'll be here before you can bury our bodies."

Kitty blinked.

"*Fine*." Suddenly defeated, Clyde slumped from his defensive stance. "Give me one second. I have to..." He pointed at his office. "The switch is in there."

"Do it." Kitty thrust a thumb at the office. Worst-case scenario, he would lock himself in like a scared teenager and they'd have to call the police and wait to be freed.

Clyde brushed past them, closing his office door behind him.

Kitty turned to Johanna in time to see the realization of the situation sink in. "There's no *handle* on the door?" Johanna whispered. "He's built a trap? What the—"

"Shh," Kitty breathed. "He's watching us on the camera up there. Let's stay calm so he doesn't do anything really stupid." She ran a hand through her hair. She had to get Johanna out of the room ASAP. "Ha," she said loudly. "Looks like I messed this meeting up, didn't I?"

Luckily, Johanna caught on without missing a beat. "Was he really horrible back then?"

"No, of course not." Kitty pretended a little laugh that sounded terribly fake to her ears. "I just tried to scare him. I've got nothing to back it up. I just want to get out and forget about Pipers."

"For sure," Johanna confirmed. "Maybe we go look at the shirts before we leave? To forget about this? I never want to think about it again, not for a moment."

A second later, the door buzzed and popped open.

Johanna reacted faster than Kitty, wedging a foot in the crack and pushing it wide.

The women hurried out, and the door closed again with a firm plop that made the hairs on Kitty's neck rise.

"Fuuuudge," Johanna muttered as they made their way to the exit past racks of evening dresses and appliqué sweaters. "In Bay Port? Are you *kidding* me?"

They only stopped when they reached the car. Kitty threw her boxes into the backseat and turned to face the music.

"I'm so sorry," she started.

But Johanna held up a hand to stop her.

Chapter 15

"What do we do?" Johanna asked.

Kitty leaned against the car. Suddenly it felt like she had soap for knee joints, making them slip any which way. "What do we do?" she repeated stupidly.

"You got us out—but how many women didn't realize it was too late before he shoved himself in their faces?" A steep line furrowed the space between Johanna's eyes. "Even if he never did a thing, he can't trap people like that. We have to do something."

"You're not angry with me?"

"I'm hopping mad." Johanna shook her hair back. "But at Clyde. Not you."

"I knew how he was, but it was so long ago I thought he'd changed." Kitty realized she was babbling as her nerves unraveled from the tight knot into which they'd twisted.

Johanna's eyes were shooting fire. "I bet you every salesperson in there has a story to tell about that man. I don't even want to know what he meant by asking for the elevator. Creep."

Kitty straightened her shoulders. "Here's what we'll do—we tell Bennett. I'm sure he's been around this block once or twice. Let's see what he says."

"Yes!" Johanna pointed triumphantly at her. "That's exactly what we'll do. Bennett will know how to handle it." She tucked her phone into her pocket. "We have evidence. Bennett likes evidence."

"Do you want to get out of here?" Kitty asked. She was desperate to get back to Bay Harbor. "I want to go home."

"Me too."

They folded themselves into the car, and Johanna whisked the Mini, tires squealing, out into the road.

Neither one of them talked until they merged onto the highway. The shops and buildings of the city center disappeared, and slowly, houses and roads were replaced by beach heather and cranberry bogs.

Kitty let down her window and leaned so the slipstream of salty air brushed her cheek, fragrant with the sap of beach pines and the dry, comforting scent of beach grass. Ospreys circled over tide zones until forest replaced the marshy fields. Then, the canopy rose high and lush and green over blueberry and huckleberry brush. With the trees forming a screen between her and the city, Kitty's heart lifted again.

"After Seal Harbor, I never thought another town would feel like home again," she said finally and turned back to her driver.

Johanna smiled at her. Leaving the city behind seemed to have the same effect on her as it had on Kitty, and her anger seemed to have evaporated. "But?"

"But Bay Harbor feels like home." Kitty smiled back. "I probably sound like a spoiled brat. I know there are many people who would love to live by the sea at all, let alone pick their favorite town."

"You loved Seal Harbor," Johanna said simply. "You lived there for a long time, and you felt safe. I understand."

Kitty spotted a bald eagle sitting high up in an old cedar, but they passed it in a moment. "Seal Harbor changed. It's not what it was. Not for me anyway," Kitty admitted. "In the end, I could barely afford to heat my house in the winter anymore. Everything was so expensive there."

Johanna kept her eyes on the road. "That's the great thing about Bay Harbor. Where else could we buy homes, let alone an entire library? We're getting in on the ground floor." She glanced at Kitty. "We're in this together."

Kitty turned back to her window. "I'm like that mistaken PI who thinks he works best alone. Having a family takes more getting used to than I thought."

Johanna hummed her understanding. "I was like that too. But there's something about the town...or maybe it's the people? It gets you good."

Kitty smiled. "The people might have something to do with it."

"Mela's trying hard to show you she cares, you know." Johanna's voice sounded careful. "I think she's worried you feel lost in all the hubbub."

Kitty didn't reply. The old resistance reared her head—she didn't want anyone to be desperate on her behalf, or pity her, or... She sighed. "It's possible I'm standing in my own way. I'm not used to people wanting to be close."

"Poor Mela. Not being close isn't a concept she understands." Johanna laughed quietly, clearly relieved Kitty saw her point, and flicked the blinker. "Better get used to it. That's all I can say to that."

They left the highway and turned into a road that became narrower at the same rate it produced bumps and potholes. Johanna slowed and let her window down too, letting her elbow rest on the bright-red frame.

Kitty leaned back. Red-winged blackbirds sang, and the breeze brushed through the tops of feathery pines as the forest receded once again. The last turn brought in sight the rugged cliffs of the coast. Beyond the drop, hugged by prongs of rocky outcroppings, the Atlantic shimmered like a blue sapphire with ever-shifting facets.

Not long after, they passed the sign announcing the town limit. "Where do you want me to drop you off?" Johanna asked.

Kitty didn't want to go to her apartment. Grateful as she was to be back, she didn't want to be alone. She didn't want to feel bad for her landlord or duck her head under the slanted roof, either. "Would you mind stopping at Mela's? I think I'll ask if I can spend the night."

Johanna glanced at her with a smile. "That's the first good idea you've had all day, Kitty."

Kitty wanted to say something clever, but then she just laughed. "I'll give you that one."

Johanna dropped her and the boxes off at twelve Seasweet Lane, waved, and drove two houses down where she pulled into her own house. Morris came out to hug her, and Johanna threw her arms around his neck and held on, burying her face in his shoulder.

Kitty sighed and walked through the riot of flowers in her sister's front yard. The door was always unlocked, but she rang the bell anyway.

It was Sunny who opened, one hand still in an oven mitt. The air coming from inside the house smelled of roasted potatoes and rosemary, rich roast in a red-wine sauce, and a hint of sweet cream and baking sheet cake.

"Kitty!" Sunny stepped aside to let her in. "Come in, honey. You're just in time for dinner."

The smells made Kitty's stomach grumble. "Hi, Sunny. Is Mela home?" Kitty set her boxes and bags down by the side table in the entrance. The walls were covered with kids' drawings and Sisley's happy abstracts.

"Hang on. I've got a cake in the oven; Amelie and I are testing—Mela?" Sunny called out on her way back into the kitchen. "Your sister is here! Can you come?"

Through the open patio doors in the living room, Kitty could see Mela in the field, surrounded by yarrow and lady's mantle and laurel, her beekeeper's hat under her arm. When she heard her aunt call, she turned and hastened through the long grass to the patio, where she tossed her veil on a chair before coming inside. "Kitty?" she called out before seeing her.

"Hi, Mela," Kitty said shyly. Not because she felt like a stranger anymore, or the poor relative, but because she'd caused the worried look on her sister's face. Mela had only ever reached out to her—but because Kitty hadn't thought herself worthy of a family, let alone a sister, she'd beat Mela's hand back.

Her sister deserved better.

She deserved better.

Mela stopped short in front of her, and Kitty opened her arms and wrapped them around her. "Hi," she murmured. "Hey, Mela."

"Hey, Kitty." Mela hugged her back, and then she stepped back to look into Kitty's eyes. "Did something happen?"

"Yes and no." Kitty folded her hands. "I'll tell you over a cup of tea if you like."

"Tea would be great. Dinner is better. I think Sunny has already set the table." A light flickered to life in Mela's eyes. "I'm so glad you have time to join us."

"In fact..." Kitty inhaled. She knew what she wanted now, but the words still didn't roll easily from her tongue. "Well, if you don't mind and if my room's still empty upstairs...I guess I was wondering if you'd mind putting up with me for a few days. The apartment is still so uncomfortable. I still haven't unpacked."

Relief softened Mela's face, and her shoulders slumped as she exhaled. "I thought you'd never ask. Of course the room's still there. It's still there, and it's all yours. I never thought the apartment was a good idea."

"I didn't want to be an inconvenience," Kitty tried to explain. Awkward and late, but Mela deserved it. "I'm too old to bother you."

"You're my *sister*." Mela blinked rapidly. "The moment I think of my only sister as an inconvenience, *I* should probably move out.

Uh. Come in. Come in." Her cheeks flushed, she waved Kitty on. "I mean, seriously, I was always afraid you'd think I... Anyway, I don't deserve this house any more than the next person."

Sunny appeared in the doorway to the kitchen, drying her hands on a tea towel. "What's wrong with you? You're talking nonsense. I hope you like chocolate nougat sheet cake with a creamy peanut butter glaze, Kitty. And cherry compote. The trees outside are going crazy this year; we can't keep up."

"I probably will like it." Kitty smiled. "Sounds delicious."

Mela exhaled. "I am talking nonsense. Come to the patio, Kitty. We're eating outside."

"Ah! Food. Finally. You both look a little pale and peckish." Sunny bustled back to the kitchen.

Kitty followed her sister outside onto the pretty stone patio with the low wall and the gorgeous ocean view and sat in the comfortable wicker chair beside Mela. The table was set with pretty, colorful plates, silverware, and crystal glasses.

"I'm pretty dense, Mela," Kitty began. "To move out when I could live here with you and Sunny at least for a while longer."

"I was starting to think you didn't like me," Mela admitted with a nervous laugh. "I loved having you, but you seemed so uncomfortable."

"Maybe it was all too much. The sale of my old place, leaving my home and losing my savings, finding a whole...a whole *family*." She spread her hands. "Family has never felt safe for me. All this—it's great. But it's a lot to take in."

"The family is yours if you want it," Mela promised. "We're pretty safe. And we're not stingy."

"No, you aren't. I was. But no more. I finally caught on."

"Relax into it," Mela suggested. "There's no need to force anything. We're here for the long run. I promise."

Footsteps interrupted them, and Amelie, followed by Sunny, joined them on the patio. They brought a golden-brown roast and steaming rosemary potatoes, green beans with walnuts and cranberries, and a spring salad with ranch dressing. Between the view and the wine and the expertly prepared food, Kitty thought it was the most delicious dinner she'd ever had.

When they were done, Amelie beamed at Kitty. "I'm so glad you came! We need your opinion. Don't anyone else dare to get up." She jumped up to collect plates and returned with a tray piled high with goodies. "I have coconut macaroons dipped in melted white chocolate, chocolate chunk scones with caramel drizzle, mini lemon meringue pies, and chocolate chip cookies with a hint of cardamom and orange zest. Oh, and sugared-rose-petal shortbread. Hmm." She eyed the tray critically. "Did I go overboard on the chocolate?"

"No," Kitty and Mela said in unison.

"But wait until you taste the sheet cake." Sunny fetched a cake stand and lifted the glass dome with a flourish. "The recipe was submitted by one of the ladies who want to work at the bakery," she said. "I'm pretty hopeful for her. Let's see."

Amelie laughed. "We already know who's going to join the team," she said. "Unlike the pie contest, the bakery is no elimination show. Can I get you a cup of tea, Kitty?"

"I can get it myself," Kitty said. "You sit down, Amelie. The tray looks delicious, but I bet you were on your feet all day baking it."

"You're a guest." Amelie made to get up, but Kitty rose quickly from her chair.

"Maybe I'm a guest, but I can still make a cup of tea as a thank-you for a fantastic dinner."

"She's going to stay for a few days," Mela said. "Besides, she's family."

"Great!" Amelie sank back with a grin. "I'll have a cup of that vanilla lavender tea, please."

When Kitty returned with the steaming teapot and a tower of cups in her hands, everyone was seated and facing the sea, chatting and laughing in the warm evening sun.

"Here we go." Kitty put down the pot and handed out cups, and then everyone helped themselves to the baked desserts. Kitty tried one of the mini lemon meringue pies. It melted in her mouth. "Mmmh." She sipped her tea and leaned back. It was easy to relax into this. How had she thought it was hard before?

"So what did you do today?" Sunny leaned forward. "Morris said you were on the road with Jo."

Kitty set down her cup and sighed. "I thought it'd be a clever idea to sell my hats at Pipers. I was sorely mistaken."

Once she started, she couldn't stop until she'd shared the entire story. Everyone listened while they ate cherry compote and drank hot tea, and when Kitty was done, the last of the weight on her chest had lifted.

"Tell Bennett." Amelie pointed her fork at Kitty. "If you don't, I will. The man's dangerous and needs to be looked at. I don't like him one bit."

"I will tell Bennett." Kitty put her cup down. "I already talked it through with Jo."

"Good. Let's hear what Bennett finds out," Mela said. "I thought you meant to sell hats again at the farmers market, Kitty?"

"I need more than the farmers market," Kitty admitted. "I'll have to open all avenues. Now that the house is sold and all that is over, I will finally have a clear head to do it."

"And you have a proper studio," Amelie said. "Maybe that'll help."

"That helps for sure," Kitty confirmed. "I actually need to get over there and finish Sisley's dress. But the kids will need the room back eventually. I hear they have a lot of requests from locals looking to rent venue space."

"By the way, Kitty, I meant to talk about something with you," Mela said haltingly. "I hope you don't take it the wrong way."

All eyes turned to her.

"Mela? What is it?" Kitty asked.

"Sam and David were sorting out Martin's things. They found his will."

Chapter 16

Kimmie washed her hands in the antique sink and dried them on the rough towel her sister swore was Portuguese linen. According to Sisley, the younger Mrs. Botrel, who ran the home goods store, had ordered it specifically for the library.

She hung the towel back and pushed open the swing door.

"All right?" Travis was waiting for her in the hall, leaning against the carved banister of the staircase.

"All right," Kimmie answered. "Let's go get Pippa."

"Pippa's with Grammy Mela until seven, I just learned." Travis pushed off to meet her. "She texted that she'll have dinner there and not to pick her up too early."

"Who texted?" Kimmie grinned and picked up her backpack from the chair. Together, they went to the front door and stepped into the glow of the evening sun. The sea behind the roofs glittered like hammered gold foil.

Travis locked the door and jumped the last step. "Pippa, of course." He chuckled. "Mela would ask. Pippa informs me."

Kimmie shook her head but knew the little girl had her dad firmly wrapped around her fingers. "So we're footloose and fancy-free. What should we do?"

They walked down Bay View toward the harbor. Somewhere between the beach roses and the honeysuckle, Travis put an arm around her and pulled her close. "Don't know," he said with a smile in his voice. "Let's go stare at the water."

"Stare at water? Nice." They made their way to the harbor, only stopping to buy ice cream before they found themselves a bench.

"There never used to be people down here," Kimmie remarked between licks of her quickly melting maple walnut ice. "Now it's becoming hard to find a bench."

Tourists in shorts and T-shirts and sundresses strolled along the water. One group of friends climbed into their moored dinghy, their hands full of ice cream cones, jugs of lemonade, and even one of the wagon-wheel blueberry pies that the tiny market on Main couldn't bake fast enough.

"Look at that." Travis pointed at a white truck farther down the harbor, toward the beach. A lengthy line was patiently waiting in front of it. "Is that the lobster truck from Beach Cove?"

Kimmy leaned forward and squinted. "It's not Gordy's," she said. "He has a red streak on his truck. He also promised Ellie never to boil a lobster again. This one also has a streak, but it's blue. I think someone took a leaf out of his book. Or it's his and he's trying to hide it from Ellie. She'll never guess it's him with a blue truck."

"I don't know a man willing to cross the women of Beach Cove." Travis finished his cone. "They know better than that, and Gordy's glad he managed to turn Ellie from an enemy into a lover once. Besides, he told Peter that he can barely run enough whale-watching tours to keep the masses calm. He has no time for making lobster rolls."

"There. It's Harris, one of Bay Harbor's own fishermen." Kimmie nodded at Harris, who had come out of the truck to kick the propane tank before disappearing again. "He's got four brothers to share into the family lobster plot, and they're all of them determined to stay in Bay Harbor."

"Good for him." Travis slouched back. "If he's getting into the lobster roll business, his brothers might be interested in whale watching. Gordy's looking for men who know their way around a boat." He held his face in the sun. "Pretty soon I'll be the only one left without a job."

Kimmie finished her ice cream too and used the paper napkin to clean her sticky fingers. "You could run a boat for Gordy," she joked.

"Ha. No. I don't think I can."

"No. You couldn't." Despite the calm waters, the fishermen at the coast of Maine had to know exactly where underwater dangers lurked. Bay Harbor was better than Beach Cove, whose idyllic cove hid many hull-rippers, but it would take Travis years to make a mediocre captain.

"I already have a career." He sighed. "You know."

Since they both were investigative journalists, Kimmie did know. The problem wasn't that Travis couldn't get work—he was good and got daily offers and requests for projects from newspapers and magazines and TV. The problem was that to do them, he'd have to leave Bay Harbor.

Kimmie didn't want him to leave. "Sisley and Morris are making their own jobs," she said softly. "So are Johanna and Kitty."

He raised an eyebrow. "I know it sounds harsh, but I don't see them earning money, either."

"Not yet, but they're positioning themselves. They will do well too," Kimmie said. "Morris has always made a living playing music. Sisley already has people touring the library asking if they can buy her paintings. Kitty earned enough with her hats in Seal Harbor, and she will do it again. And Johanna will have fun doing her readings and book clubs. She's started to write fiction too, but that's still a badly kept secret. Don't tell anyone. Though I think maybe you're the last to know. Well, maybe Mom. Johanna doesn't want Mom to organize a reading for her quite yet."

"Huh."

Kimmie stirred. "Hey. Wake up."

"What?" He opened one eye to look at her, then both, then sat up. "Sorry. I've been schlepping books all day, and Pippa didn't sleep well last night. Her nose was stuffy. I think she's allergic to something that's blooming around the house right now."

"We should talk seriously about the job thing," Kimmie said. "I want to stay here."

"You want to stay here?" He smiled. "As in, forever?"

"Forever is a long time, but maybe? Who knows? I want to stay until... Well, if everything's going according to plan, we'll need to settle down for a few years. Possibly eighteen to twenty. We can't do that on savings."

He looked at her. "Everything will go according to plan, Kimmie. Don't worry."

"I've never wanted three months to pass so badly! I didn't think I'd be so invested, but..."

He chuckled. "I'm glad you are invested. It's not that much longer to go. And if you want to tell your mom earlier—that's fine too. In fact, I'm all for it."

Kimmie put a hand on her belly.

Planned or not, now that the test had come back positive, she couldn't imagine losing the tiny baby forming inside her. But Travis had caught it even worse—he seemed in complete denial about the simple statistical fact that a lot could go wrong in the first three months.

"So anyway, we need jobs," she resumed her earlier train of thought. "Like proper parents." She expanded her lungs for her next words. "You know, I think I should sell the apartment in the city."

He sat upright. "Your city apartment? Are you serious?"

She held up her open palms. "We need the money but not the apartment, right? I just bought a whole house. I'm pregnant, and I want my kid to grow up here, where she can swing looking out at the sea and where she's surrounded by family."

Travis turned to look at the sea. "Your kid?"

"Ours." She cleared her throat. She hadn't realized he was so sensitive about it, but after all they'd been through, it made sense. "We should probably talk about a couple of big-picture things."

He looked back, and she was relieved to see the warmth in his eyes. "Yes," he said simply. "It's overdue."

Kimmie waited for a moment. When it became evident that neither one of them knew how to start, she smiled. "Well?"

His chest expanded. "Well—for starters, do you want me around for the long haul? Obviously, things change when children are involved."

Kimmie frowned. Had she misread everything about their relationship? She lowered her gaze to her hands. Already, her fingers were nervously trailing around her nail beds, ready to start picking. It was a childhood thing she'd never gotten rid of. She balled her fingers into fists and tucked them under her legs for safekeeping. "I wish you wouldn't feel the need to ask."

His eyes met hers. "Is that a yes?"

"It's a yes from me. It's always been yes, Travis. Don't you know that?"

He leaned over and kissed her forehead. She closed her eyes and drew in the warm scent of his skin.

He slumped and ran his hands through his hair. "I meant to ask you each and every morning waking next to you. But I was too much of a coward." The breath leaving his chest shook with pent-up emotion. "I behaved like a coward when I left you, and I'm a coward coming back. I don't mind driving a beat-up, stolen jeep into the center of a war zone, but when it comes to you, I'm scared. I don't deserve you."

Kimmie warmed as the meaning of his words reached her. "You're scared because you love me."

"I love you. Always, always." He dropped his hands. "Kimmie, I cannot tell you how much I appreciate your generosity. No other woman would have given me a second chance after what I did."

Everything inside Kimmie lifted, and sang, and jubilated. The question had weighed on her as well. "I love you too," she replied, feeling her lips curve. "I'm the one who loves you too. Maybe that's why."

His eyes shimmered. "Maybe that's why," he said, his voice tender. He held out his hand, and she gave him hers.

For a long while, they sat side by side, watching the cormorants on the buoys drying their wings in the sinking sun. They didn't say another word until the evening had kissed the gold off the water and the waves lapped against the stones like velvet and ink.

The burning need to talk it out, to plan and decide, had left Kimmie's chest. She now knew what the big picture was—they loved each other as much or more than before the divorce. Everything else would fall into place. They could sell their other places, they could start a local newspaper, they could think of other things to do. Pippa and the bean would grow up here, in a small peaceful seaside town full of friends and family.

"It's getting cool, isn't it?" Travis rose and pulled her with him. "We should pick up Pippa too."

Kimmie slipped her arm around him. Despite the night breeze, he was warm. "Maybe we'll tell Mom after all. What do you think?"

She felt his gaze on her. "Are you sure?"

Now that the worry had left and only the baby occupied her belly, things were different. "Yes," Kimmie said. "But let's do it properly. Next time the family is together."

He laughed. "As you wish. Oy vey." He kissed the top of her head, and she snuggled under his arm. Together, they walked to their car, which was parked in the harbor lot, and drove home.

Chapter 17

"Lift your arm." The words sounded more like *fif your farm* because Kitty had needles clamped between her lips so she could use her hands to tighten the waist of the wedding dress.

Sisley did as she was told. Not following her aunt's orders promptly could result in pinpricks, she'd learned earlier. "What do you think?" She couldn't see herself in the massive ornate mirror they'd dragged from the upstairs powder room into Kitty's atelier.

Kitty stepped back, lowering her reading glasses with a critical frown. "Do not lose any more weight," she ordered. "Or we'll get in all sorts of trouble with the seams. It won't line up properly if I make it tighter."

"Got it." Sisley still didn't know what she looked like. Not too good, judging from Kitty's cragged brow. "Can I?" She pointed longingly at the mirror.

"It's not finished, and your hair looks like you rode a seahorse to the fitting."

"Please?"

"Oh, all right. Go ahead." Kitty pushed the remaining pins into her tomato pin cushion, but Sisley caught her glancing over to catch her reaction.

She smiled. It wasn't so important how the dress looked—already it felt like a cloud and was made with love. Like all brides in love, she wanted to look stunning for Bennett. But deep down, she knew her dress wouldn't make a difference. Already, she'd glimpsed tears in his eyes when he talked about their simple church wedding. Paired with his inability to tell silk from polyester, she could wear a fleece onesie and he'd take her.

Her heart fluttered as she positioned herself before the mirror, imagining walking down the church aisle toward him. Then she looked up. "Oh."

A fairy looked back at her. Her blonde hair was tousled and fell over her shoulders as if, like Kitty said, she'd ridden a seahorse to the fitting. But the dress...

Sisley turned from side to side, letting her grandmother's skirt swing wide. A gust from the open window picked it up, and she spun around, letting the fine material float like a princess skirt from a fairy tale. When she stopped, arms spread wide, the fabric swished back into place with the sound of pearls falling into wild grass. "Oooh!" she sighed. "I love it."

"*Careful.*" Kitty had given up pretense and was standing behind Sisley, hands on hips. "It's only pinned, kiddo."

"Oh, Kitty." Sisley put her hands on her waist. The dress made it look tiny. She'd been pregnant so long and forever wearing Julie's loose hippie dresses and tunics afterward; she'd forgotten she *had* a waist. And the top was so delicate and feminine...

Stretching her neck, she let a finger trail over the delicate lace that hugged her throat and made her look as slim and fragile as porcelain when she was anything but.

"Is it scratchy?"

Sisley shook her head. "I can barely feel it at all. It's like..." She searched for words. "Like a leaf you put on your hand before you blow it off and make a wish," she concluded.

"That's the first I hear of leaves granting wishes." But in the mirror, Sisley saw that her aunt was well pleased with the comparison. "Did you see the heart?" Kitty asked.

Sisley checked her wrist. Below the lace shimmered the small blue heart, cut from her sister's wedding dress. She put her hand over it, pressing it into the underside of her arm where it was most tender. "Perfect. Something blue."

"Ready for the belt?"

"Yes." Sisley lifted her arms, and her aunt slung the glittering, jeweled belt around her, tying the strings in the back.

Her aunt was smiling at Sisley's reflection when she stepped back. "Well? What do you think?"

"I can't." Sisley felt the intricate pattern of stones and beads. They were hard and beautiful, and they made her waist look even smaller.

Kitty's eyes found hers in the mirror. "You don't like it?"

"Oh! I love it," Sisley whispered. Then she took a breath. "I love it, Kitty," she repeated. "It's like it's growing right into me. Reaching its roots through my skin and wrapping its vines around my insides. It's actually making me a little dizzy."

Kitty shook her head, but she was smiling. "Growing into you? That's the first time I heard someone say that about a dress. Does it hurt?"

Sisley shook her head. "No. It feels wonderful."

Her aunt's eyes shone. "I'm glad. I wanted it to feel wonderful."

Kitty went over to where Sisley's straw tote sat on the table and pulled out a hairbrush. "Now, let's see how it looks with your hair right. I was thinking it'd be good to pull your hair up to show off the lace." She began to run the brush through Sisley's hair, bringing order to the blonde strands.

"Mmmh." Sisley closed her eyes, enjoying the sensation. "I didn't know wearing a dress could make me feel this good."

"Imagine walking down the aisle in it to meet Bennett."

"Don't. I'll start crying." Already, her vocal cords trembled. Sisley sniffled, hoping she wouldn't cry and leave a stain on the silk of the skirt. Blinking, she looked at the ceiling. "I thought I didn't care what I wore." A watery laugh wriggled loose. "I mean, I still don't. But if I have to wear anything at all, this is it."

"I promise you have to wear something. And if it's the right dress, you care. I don't know why. But I've seen it with hats too. Not always but quite often."

Kitty twisted strands this way and that, pinning with the pearl clams Sisley had found in a little store in Beach Cove. Her faint perfume—or maybe it was just her natural smell—made Sisley think of light-green linen and silk looking like the Atlantic in spring.

"Now look." The scent disappeared and reappeared together with a tissue.

Sisley dabbed at her eyes. She barely recognized herself in the mirror. "So elegant," she whispered. "How did you do that?" She turned, the skirt swishing softly and dropping again with the sound of pearls falling in a meadow.

Kitty too had a tissue in her hand. The frown from earlier had long disappeared. "I'm glad you like it, Sisley," she said. "You're beautiful. That's what's doing it."

"I love the way all three dresses came together." Sisley had to turn back and look again. She wasn't vain, but this moment of standing here and discovering this new person in the old mirror would never come again.

Behind her, Kitty murmured something. Sisley looked over her shoulder. "What did you say?"

"Lace, silk, beads. Smooth, soft, and tough. Just like you, my dear. You love it so much because it's the perfect fit for you."

Smooth, soft, and tough. It was the nicest compliment Sisley had ever gotten, and like the dress itself, it touched her soul. "Thank you." She laughed and dabbed her eyes at the same time. "I'm so happy you made this for me. Never in a lifetime could I have found a dress like this at a store. You're a magician with the needle, Kitty."

"Oh well." Kitty had gotten over her soft moment, and her laugh was quite cheerful. "It's just three old dresses cut up and pinned together. But seeing how much you like it does make me happy.

Now, step out of it again, honey. I think we'll stitch it together like this, don't you?"

"My heart will break if you change a single thing." Sisley turned her back to Kitty, who started to undo the pearl buttons.

It took a while, even though Kitty's nimble fingers were flying.

"Kitty?" Sisley asked after a while.

"Yes?"

"Could I try on one of your hats?"

"The hats?" More buttons fell open.

Sisley held up the dress. She was wearing a silk slip underneath that had been a gift from Johanna. She'd also brought Julie's faded kimono robe in case she would feel naked in front of her aunt, but the robe had stayed in the little pouch Sunny had stitched together as a Christmas present for Sisley.

"Yes. You're a great seamstress. I wonder how it feels to wear one of your hats. That's your real talent, isn't it?"

"I think so."

"Well, I'd love to wear one after the dress turned out so perfect."

Kitty lowered the dress for Sisley to step out of, careful to keep any loosened pin ends away from her skin. "Well, the thing is, though, darling, you didn't *order* a hat."

Sisley leaned against the desk and watched her aunt drape the dress over a dress form. Why did she have to order a hat? There were hats sitting on the shelf. Was her hair not freshly washed and clean? "I don't wear hats," she tried to explain. "I didn't mean to order one. I just want to see how it feels wearing something you made with your special talent."

Kitty glanced at the top of her head. The look was as nimble and skilled as her fingers. "I understand. But that's not how it works. You have to order one," she said. "Specifically a straw boater to protect your skin when you're painting in the field by the sea. Your grandmother Julie would give you one if she could."

It was such a strange statement that Sisley wrapped her arms around herself. "What?"

"I'll make you one." Kitty narrowed her eyes, squinting at Sisley's head. "But not yet. I'll have it ready for August. You should have it in August."

"Okay. Ha. I didn't know that's how it works." Sisley stepped behind the trifold and quickly changed into her shorts and loose blouse, then stepped into her canvas shoes.

"Hey," Kitty called out suddenly. "Just to clarify, is that what you wanted? A boater for painting in the field?"

Sisley smiled. Her aunt had been caught in a work trance. Sisley knew the feeling. She also knew the feeling of sometimes just knowing what a painting needed to look like. She even knew what it felt like when Julie left a sudden message though she couldn't be sure Kitty received them the same way.

She stepped out from the trifold, rolling up her sleeves. "A boater is exactly what I want, especially when a boater is what I think it is. Can you make Bennett a hat too?"

"If he wants one, he'll have to come talk to me," Kitty said, leaning close to the dress form and pinning something. "Otherwise I'll end up making him a bowler. He's so proper, but I doubt he'd wear a bowler hat."

Sisley tilted her head, amused. Obviously, Kitty had a special relationship with her hats—and possibly her customers.

Kitty caught her smile. "Custom-made, remember?" She chuckled. "It's just how I do it. Not at the farmers market, of course, but family gets the real deal."

The breeze lifted and rustled the draped silk. Sisley stepped to the window to close it, casting a look at the sidewalk downstairs. The library door was propped open, and a handful of curious locals had stopped by to have a look. Some of them could be heard inside; others were standing outside, their small groups of neighbors and friends spilling onto the cobbled street.

Bennett would never come to let his head be measured for a hat he didn't want. But someone else would. "You know who asked me about your hats?"

"Who?"

"The woman who runs the home goods store, Maison de Sand."

Kitty rose from her crouched position and pressed a hand into her lower back. "Oof. The old lady from Brittany?"

"Her daughter-in-law, Annie Botrel. She's had a bit of bad luck lately. She said she could use a nice hat to cheer her up."

"Really?"

"In fact, she's standing down there." Sisley held the window open. "Do you want me to call her up?"

Kitty straightened, then glanced at the window. "She'll just want to talk," she said. "If she wanted to buy, she'd have come to me, not you."

"She's interested, Kitty. Why be shy now? You want them to talk about your hats. Even if they don't buy. Some of them will."

"Hmm, maybe."

"She's right downstairs," Sisley insisted. "I can go bring her up. Come on, it's how you really work. One-on-one, talking it out until you know what's best and then seeing your creation worn in town. Not making a bunch of berets for Pipers. Am I right?"

Finally, Kitty nodded. "Okay. It's as good a day to start as any other."

Chapter 18

"Thank you for owning the most comfortable chairs in the world." Kitty let herself sink into the crackling wicker. It was just her and her sister tonight in the little blue house. Sunny was at Amelie's big new house. The pie contest had started, and the semi-finale no-bake cake judging round was happening in the kitchen.

"Busy day?" Mela crackled her own chair as she picked up her gin and tonic and pushed Kitty's closer.

Kitty took a sip. "Tastes like the juniper berries were picked right here at the coast." She sighed happily. "Yes, busy day. Good day, though. Sisley's happy with her dress."

"Happy is an understatement. She was over the moon. I wanted to thank you for doing this for her. I don't often see her so excited." Mela pulled on the cable-knit sweater she'd brought outside.

At the coast, June nights could still be cool. But at least there was no breeze tonight, and they could have candles on the patio table and the old stone wall.

For a while, they talked about Sunny's contest. Far from seeming exhausted by all the commotion, Mela's aunt seemed unstoppable, gathering speed as she went along.

"We should talk about Martin's will," Kitty said after the topic of fruit fillings was exhausted. "We need to decide what to do with the store and the house."

"Both are exactly as he left them. I drove to Beach Cove to make sure things are okay for now. I brought his spider plant home." She looked down, watching the ice float in her glass. "It's eerie to be in his house without him."

"It's a beautiful house, though. I always loved being in there."

"It is one of the old fishing cottages. He built it out and took care of it."

"And the store?"

Mela shook her head. "Everyone in Beach Cove knows why the store is closed, but the tourists are trickling in from New Jersey and Massachusetts. They put up notes on the door, asking for Martin to call them with the new opening hours."

"Oh no."

"And they left so many messages on Martin's ancient answering machine it ran out of tape. I listened to them. Some of them bought their saltwater taffy at the store since they were kids."

"They'll miss him."

"They'll miss their taffy," Mela amended.

"Should we read his will now? I think I'm ready."

"Yeah? It'd be a good time, with everyone else out of the house."

"Can you imagine? I was always alone."

"Yes, let's do it. It's time to take care of the house and the store." Kitty sipped her drink, listening to Mela going into the house and pulling the envelopes from the drawer in the kitchen. Back outside, she handed Kitty the one addressed to her before she sat back down.

Kitty set her glass down. The alcohol warmed her hands and cheeks, but the beating of her heart had to do with the envelopes. "We both get a copy?"

Mela nodded. "The attorney sent us one each. I suppose he still had that address on file for you from when you first moved to Bay Harbor."

"I never told him I moved." Kitty picked up the envelope. "Do you know what it says?"

Mela shook her head. "I wanted to wait for you so we could read it together. Hey..." She held out a hand. "Whatever Martin wants—I don't need anything more than I have."

Kitty grasped her hand and squeezed it briefly. "You have kids, Mela. Grandchildren. They have rights too. And I don't need charity."

Mela picked up her envelope as well. "Let's see what he wants before we start haggling. Maybe all he left us is a heap of debts."

"Hmm." Just the thought left Kitty unable to speak.

They opened their letters, both leaning toward the flickering light of the candle to read their grandfather's last will.

It didn't take very long. Martin was very clear.

"Well." Mela folded her copy back up and pushed it back into the envelope. "I thought I had a pretty good idea, but that's more than I expected."

Kitty couldn't think. She sat with her paper in her hand, staring into the dark.

"You all right?" Mela rose and picked up their glasses. "I'd much rather have Martin back, but since that's not possible... Shall we have another drink to the will? We're wealthy women now. Beach Cove real estate was always expensive, and it has shot up even higher lately."

Kitty nodded. She was still feeling numb.

Mela left and Kitty sat in the garden, listening to the rushing of the waves and the whispering grass. Somewhere, a great horned owl hooted.

It was the most comforting sound in the world.

Kitty counted the deep, hollow calls until her shoulders relaxed and her breath came easily. Then she looked back at the paper. She couldn't quite make out the words without leaning to the candles, but already, she knew them by heart.

I give you and your sister equally my house and the candy store and everything else I own. Do what you think is best. I don't ask that you keep the store running—that was my task. Don't let the fishermen and their wives talk you into selling candy apples and licorice, either if it won't make you happy. I love you both. My last wish is that you do what makes your heart sing.

There was more—the lawyer's notes listing the assets, the approximate value of the house and the store and the bank accounts.

Ice clinked on glass in the kitchen. Soon after, Mela returned and handed Kitty a glass. "To Martin." She held out hers.

Kitty rose as well to clink her glass against her sister's. "To Martin. The sweetest man who ever walked the coast of Maine."

"It'll be easier now," Mela said softly. "The loss of your house in Seal Harbor won't matter so much."

Kitty nodded and they drank. It was a lot to take in. There was the relief over the money, the fact that she'd much rather have Martin back, and the weird feeling that none of it was real. "What smells so good?" Kitty asked, just to say something.

"That's the trumpet honeysuckle over there." Mela walked over to where the patio widened and showed Kitty where the gnarled wooden trunk of a honeysuckle crept along the stonewall. It must have been there as long as the house, Kitty thought, and it was covered with hundreds of flowers, their rich scarlet red visible in the starlight. A little further, Kitty could make out the bright, heavy heads of peonies, each glowing like a soft, petaled moon.

"My mother had her honeybees here. She planted the honeysuckle herself, but the linden tree was already here. The honeybees love its fragrance. And the nectar. It's practically dripping with it." Mela walked on and was standing below a tall tree, silhouetted against the sea. "Smell the air."

Now Kitty noticed the sweet linden flowers as well. She sat on the wall. The rough stones were still warm from the day. A cloud shifted, and the moonlight reflected off their surface, catching the soft moss growing on them. It felt downy under her hand, the way she imagined the owl hooting in the distance felt.

"What do you think about Martin's will?" Mela asked, bringing Kitty back from the romance of the night to the reality of life. "He's left us a lot of money."

"I've never had anyone give me money. Let alone a lot of it. I don't know how I feel right now."

"Then you might as well feel good."

Her footsteps crunched on the patio stones, and a moment later, Mela sat on the wall beside Kitty, swinging her legs over the other side so she could see the ocean.

Kitty followed her example. The water glittered white and silver in the moonlight. The waves changed shape and speed like willful horses, prancing here and there, driven by invisible currents deep underwater despite the windless night. Nobody could ever get bored watching it.

"Money and love and sweet summer nights." Mela sighed. "I wish everyone could have an endless supply."

"Wouldn't that be just the thing?"

"You know what I can't quite wrap my brain around? The fact that Martin loved us." Mela picked a lavender blossom and rubbed it between her fingers. The fragrance mingled with the honeysuckle and the salt of the sea. "It was such a surprise to find out he was my grandfather. It makes sense my family should be strewn around the area, I guess. But I didn't even know Finn was my dad."

"I've known Martin all my life even if I wasn't always able to have contact with him." Kitty put a foot on the wall and wrapped her arms around her knee.

For a while, they were silent. Then Mela said, "He told you to do what makes your heart sing. Anything you want: travel the world, work to change the lives of others, or do nothing."

"He told you the same."

"I'm already doing what I want. But what do you want from life? Do you want to move back to Seal Harbor?"

Kitty smiled. "If we sell Martin's house and store and you give me your portion, I might finally afford a basement studio there."

"Rub elbows with the rich and famous? Sound good?"

"I'm not going back. I finally found out that I like my coast rugged and my streets smelling fishy."

"You could live in Martin's house," Mela said suddenly. "No more tiny apartment with slanted ceilings. And we could turn the candy store into a hat store. A proper atelier. It has enough windows."

"Live in Beach Cove?" Kitty exhaled. "But..."

"But?"

Kitty had to laugh at herself. "But all my family is here in Bay Harbor," she said. "I just made up my mind to stick with you."

"Oh good. Not that Beach Cove is so far, but I'd rather have you in town," Mela said. "So we sell Martin's house and get you something here. I think between all of us, we've bought enough real estate to raise prices even in Bay Harbor, but it's still much cheaper than Beach Cove."

"Hmm. I'm not sure. It'd be such a pity to lose the house and store to strangers too." Kitty loved the charming old candy store, and Martin's house was in easy walking distance. It was an expanded cottage from the eighteen hundreds with a sweet garden in the back where Martin had grown roses and sat under his own linden tree. Like the tree branching over the hives, it would be dripping now with the abundant nectar the yellow-green blossoms produced in June.

"The good thing is, we don't have to decide now." Mela stretched her arms in the air and yawned. "We'll sleep on it for a week or two. It will come to us."

"Is Peter coming over?"

"He's manning the registration tonight." Mela swung her legs back, and Kitty followed her. "But Charlie is interviewing people for the job tomorrow. Hopefully they find someone they like so

Peter and Charlie can go home and sleep at night again." She shook her head.

"What about all the other jobs they need help with?" They grabbed their letters and glasses in passing, and Kitty blew out the candles in their hurricane lamps.

"Also interviewing tomorrow. Charlie says he wants the two of them to be free so they can get going on the mill."

"What mill?"

"Didn't I tell you? They're turning the old mill by the cranberry bog into a new bakery."

They walked inside and locked the patio door behind them, and even though they were tired from the long, sunny day, they couldn't make themselves go to bed. Instead, they curled up with blankets and ice cream and put on a movie that made them laugh until Sunny came home and scolded them into bed like a pair of wayward teenagers.

Kitty grabbed a quick shower and then snuggled into the soft flannel sheets of her bed. Outside the window, the stars twinkled as steady as the waves lapped against the coast, and when she finally closed her eyes, Kitty thought a dream about finding out what made her heart sing was already waiting.

Chapter 19

The younger Mrs. Botrel—Annie was her name—was pretty. She was in her forties and had two teenage sons at home in Beach Cove. Her face was rather wide but pleasing, and her expressive mouth made it interesting. Though right now, the lips pressed into a tight line and the brown eyes unsuccessfully blinked back tears.

"Here." Kitty pushed the tissue box across the table.

"Thanks." Annie Botrel pulled out a tissue and blew her nose. "I'm sorry."

"Come sit down." Kitty pulled out a chair for her new client. They'd been talking standing up, but clearly, Annie had hit a sudden snag telling Kitty about herself. "Can I get you a cup of tea, or water, or anything else?"

Annie waved the hand holding the tissue impatiently in the air. "Thanks, but I'm good. I'll just...sit down." She did, putting her purse on the floor and one jeans-clad leg over the other. A moment later, she lowered the tissue and smiled a watery apology. "Sorry."

"No. No worries." Kitty didn't often have clients cry, but it happened now and then when Kitty asked about themselves. Sometimes, Kitty didn't even have to do that much. Just having a moment to think about themselves could trigger a crying spell.

In those cases, Kitty's job was to find out why—and make a hat that helped make the wearer feel better.

Calmly, Kitty took the chair opposite. "Is it anything I can help you with?"

Annie shook her head and dabbed her eyes. The apologetic smile firmed into embarrassment, and then she laughed nervously. "I didn't mean to bring this to you, I promise. Only..."

"Deep breath." Kitty smiled back. She was here for these stories. They helped her create good hats—the hidden truths, the stories waiting in the dark and lonely corners of the mind. Kitty couldn't change them.

But she could give a sad woman a bright hat band or a woman who felt stuck a beautiful feather. She'd made a tiny leather heart to represent courage for a young teacher with a rowdy class and flowers to symbolize growth and beauty for a woman scared to turn forty. For an administrator who always felt her dream job was just out of reach, Kitty had twisted twine into the shape of a dreamcatcher. For a bullied teenager, she'd sewn a princess diadem of pearls into the inside of a fedora, and a bubbly newlywed distraught over her first marital spat received colorful ribbons to remind her of the vibrancy of her life. The list was endless.

Annie's chest heaved once. "We own two home goods stores."

"Maison de Sand in Beach Cove, and Maison de Mer here in Bay Harbor. I love your stores. Everybody does."

A smile tugged on Annie's lips. "Thank you. Anyway, a while ago a new store opened in Sandville. It's a big chain of home goods. A very big chain. We're a small local business. We can't match their selection, never mind the prices." She tugged on a strand of her auburn hair. "Well, ever since that happened..."

"They draw your business?"

Mrs. Botrel nodded. "At first we thought we'd be okay. We offer higher quality. Everything is handmade or at least handpicked... We figured it wouldn't be so bad." Her face clouded. "We tried, but it's no good. For a while we absorbed the damage, but it caught up with us. My husband wants to get rid of the Bay Harbor store. But that store is *my* baby. *I* opened it, and I really—I *really*—" She sniffled.

"You really like it?"

A deep sigh lifted her chest. "Yes. I really like it. I wanted so badly to create a cozy atmosphere in the store, filling it with homey scents and comforting music. It seems to me Bay Harbor needs a store like that. I meant it to become a regular shopping stop for the community, where customers come to browse and chat because they feel welcomed, appreciated, and inspired." She cleared her throat.

"I'll admit that it was a competition with my husband running the store in Beach Cove. A friendly competition, but still... I was always at a disadvantage because Beach Cove is overrun with tourists and Bay Harbor is not. But I was so sure I could do well. Not even my husband knows this, but I secretly hoped to turn my small shop into a boutique. I hoped to sell more than tea towels and egg cups. Maybe locally made purses and jewelry. It seems silly now, but I even dreamed of selling braided rugs and a lamp or a kitchen table set here and there. In fact, I was stupid enough to keep a list of pretty things I wanted to sell. If wishes were fishes, huh?"

Kitty had listened without interrupting. "It'd be wonderful to have a store like that in Bay Harbor. We wouldn't have to bring all our business to Bay Port—or send the money off into the internet. I prefer to buy local."

"Exactly." Annie Botrel shook her head. "But it's unrealistic. The bills are piling up well past the point where selling a dish towel a day will do. My eldest will look at colleges this year."

Kitty couldn't imagine the pressure of providing for a child. Often enough it felt like she couldn't even provide for herself.

"He's not reaching for the stars. But even going to Bay Port University is expensive." Annie lifted her hands in a gesture of defeat. "I thought we were finally getting somewhere. That all the hard work was paying off. Instead, we're backpedaling. Closing the second store that was supposed to pay for the boys' education."

She frowned and pulled another tissue from the box. This time, her movement was angry, not sad.

Kitty waited for a moment, but Annie seemed to have talked herself out.

"Do you just want to forget about the hat?" Kitty asked eventually. "It's not cheap. I wish I could do it for free, but my business is in a spot of trouble too. I know a thing or two about mass-produced competition. Amazon sells hats for pennies, delivered to your door."

"I'm sorry to hear that!" The legs uncrossed, and Annie sat up straight. "But that's not what I meant at all. My mother-in-law would be furious if I didn't get this hat. Then she'll make fish soup."

"Fish soup?" Kitty smiled.

A pained look narrowed Annie's eyes. "Bouillabaisse. It's her comfort food; she claims it calms her down. My husband loves it too. I can't stand it. I pretended I did when she first moved in because I adore my mother-in-law. Now I can't admit I've lied all along." The corners of her mouth lifted in another small smile. "We make soap together, you know. It turns out better when you're fond of each other."

"I've noticed the soap. It smells divine." Kitty rose. "I've started a design for you after seeing you at the counter in your store. You looked so happy wrapping up a tablecloth into gift paper."

"It was a floral table runner, one hundred percent flax linen imported from Italy. You can't help but be happy when you touch it." Her lips curved fully. "I saw you too."

"The hat is not at all done. It takes me about eight hours to make it," Kitty explained as she went to the shelf to find what she'd started. "Some clients think I have a stack of raw models and just trim them. But I start from scratch every time." Kitty scanned the shelves for the hat box she'd picked for Annie. "For you, I took a hat body of raw beaver felt and blocked it to your size. I was glad to find I had your measurements right."

"Oh."

"Next I cut it, but I want your opinion. What do you like?" Kitty shoved the footstool where she needed it and stepped on it to reach the box. She pulled it out of the shelf and brought it to the table.

Annie tucked her chin and pursed her pretty lips. "I like a hint of a Western hat," she decided. "But not so much brim that I look like a cowboy."

Kitty wiggled the round lid off the box and pulled out the blocked felt. "How do you like the color?"

Surprise flickered over the store owner's face. "Oooh," she murmured. "I love it! It's the color of summer lavender just beginning to dry out. How did you know?" She ran her fingers over the felt, admiring the soft shade of purple.

"It wasn't so hard to guess." Lavender tints dotted both home goods stores like the recurring theme of a symphony.

"So now what?" Annie Botrel held on to the felt. It meant the hat and Kitty's client were off to a good start.

"Now I shape it, and then I make it pretty. Do you have any requests?"

Annie shook her head. "Only that you do it yourself. I trust your taste."

Kitty flushed warmly. Old as she was, her clients' trust never failed to have an effect on her. "Thank you."

She unfolded a silk cloth on the old library desk and asked Annie to set the felt on it. Then she pointed at the different areas of it as she explained what came next. "I'll sand and iron the crown, fold and adjust the brim, do a couple of other things to make sure it fits and sew in a sweatband... And then comes the fun part where I add the bells and whistles that make it uniquely yours." She looked up and couldn't help but smile at Annie's expectant expression.

"What are you going to do?"

"It will come to me as I shape the hat. But I promise you'll have the only one of its kind."

"Who wouldn't like to wear something unique?" Annie rose.

If Kitty hadn't seen it, she wouldn't be able to tell the woman had cried only moments before. Now, her eyes and smile were as cloudless as the summer sky that dried her lavender.

"Can I pick it up tonight before I drive back to Beach Cove? I won't be back in Bay Harbor this week."

Kitty eyed the clock on the wall. "I'll text you when it's ready. To be honest, it's going to be a close call—we don't want to risk it losing its shape because I rushed it."

"No, of course not." The lips dropped with disappointment.

"If it's not today, I'll drive over tomorrow and drop it off."

"You don't have to do that. I can get it next week."

"No, I think you should have it sooner," Kitty decided. "Besides, it's no trouble—I have to visit Beach Cove anyway." She followed her guest to the stairs. She wanted to look in on the store and Martin's cottage. There was no reason not to do it tomorrow. She felt in her gut that this hat needed to be made and delivered by the morning.

"Oh. Before I forget." One foot on the stair step, Annie stopped short. "Do you know what will happen to the candy store? Some of the tourists have bought their taffy from Martin since they were kids, and they come to the store just to ask my husband. Bruno misses Martin a lot, and he's becoming depressed having to repeat over and over that his good friend has passed away. Should we put a note on the door?"

"I will. Not sure what I'll write on it though, since I don't know yet what we'll do with it," Kitty admitted. "My sister and I inherited it, and we're trying to figure it out. Maybe it will come to me while I finish your hat. If it does, I'll tell you when I see you tomorrow."

Chapter 20

Still sleepy from working late the night before, Kitty lowered Annie Botrel's hat into the lined hat box, then stood back for a last look.

It had turned out as she'd hoped. The hat clearly belonged to the sweet store owner. If someone would find it on a sidewalk, they'd carry it over to the store, assuming it was the younger madame who lost it.

Over time, Kitty had learned to switch off thinking and feel her way forward when trimming hats. The important part was to think of the person who would wear it.

She stepped back to admire the effect of the silk paper on her creation. The soft felt was trimmed with delicate floral lace colored the opaque plum of a summer night sky. Tiny barely visible sequins sewn into the lace reflected the dreams and hopes Annie hid between soaps and fabrics in her lavender stores. Still, the sequins would glint in the sun when least expected, making people turn their heads for a second look and a smile. Kitty figured a busy mother and wife, shop owner and soap-pourer could use a second look and a smile sometimes.

There was more to the hat, but the morning sun was turning the rosy morning sky brighter and bluer by the minute. Kitty had no time to lose. She closed the box.

First, she had to drop off the hat in Beach Cove, then she wanted to have a look at the house and the store to help make up her mind.

Last but not least, she was determined to be back by noon to wash her hair and change.

Even though the renovations in the library were still ongoing, Morris and Sisley were ready.

All the stairs were tested for their weight limits, the floorboards for their carrying capacity, holes had been closed and windows washed. Cleaning supplies and leftover construction materials had been tucked away in the back rooms; all the chandelier bulbs worked—in short, it was time for the official grand opening.

The mayor would come and cut the ribbon in the early afternoon. After that, the town folks, fingers crossed, would come to the first event—a gallery showing upstairs and a jazz concert downstairs.

Johanna was going to use the occasion to drum up a book club and spread the word about some author readings she was planning.

Kitty still felt guilty about bringing Johanna to Pipers department store—or more accurately, to the waiting room with no door handle.

They had told Bennett about the incident and learned that it was called false imprisonment to lock someone in a room against their will. It was a felony and carried hefty charges if they reported it and Clyde was found guilty.

After talking it through over plenty of charcuterie, wine and cheese, Kitty and Johanna decided not to pursue legal action, only because Clyde opened the door when they asked. Instead, Kitty sent a letter to the owner of Pipers, attaching Johanna's cell phone video and describing what had happened. If the owner was any good, it should be enough to look into Clyde's behavior and prevent more women from getting trapped in the waiting room.

A few days later, the owner wrote back, sincerely apologizing for the inconvenience. The letter was carefully worded. Maybe old Mrs. Piper was scared of a lawsuit, maybe she was genuinely appalled. Whichever it was, she wrote that after she read the letter, she had driven straight into Bay Port and marched straight into the waiting room. When she found a gleaming door handle on the shabby door and saw the unauthorized camera, she had fired Clyde Carsten on the spot.

There had been a wake of complaints from the employees who witnessed the firing, and Mrs. Piper lost no time confiscating Clyde's computer so he couldn't mess with it. She ordered a third-party team to dig through the video footage he'd stored on it. If there was something unsavory to see, she meant to stare it in the eye. In short, Mrs. Piper, in all the glory of her eighty-six years, was hopping mad. The man had besmirched her beloved store's good name. If there was evidence, even if Johanna and Kitty wouldn't report him to the police, she certainly would. For sure.

Kitty left the library, waving at Travis and Kimmy who were sitting on the stairs in the morning sun, waiting for the rest of the crew to arrive while sharing a breakfast of an orange juice and a croissant.

One croissant. Between the two of them.

Kitty took the corner to go to the parking lot in the back when she heard Travis coax Kimmie into taking just one bite. Just one. Crackers were supposed to help. Maybe a croissant would too.

Kitty smiled to herself as she pulled out onto the narrow road. Unless she was mistaken, the couple had a little surprise in store for Mela.

The drive over the cliff was beautiful. Whatever morning mist still hung in the Bay Harbor pines was gone by the time Kitty crossed over into Beach Cove. Not long after she passed the highest point of the cliff, Kitty spotted Sam's pickup truck parked by the side of the road.

Parking at the marina and walking up into town, Kitty texted Annie and asked whether she wanted to meet for a coffee at the marketplace café. Annie wanted, and they sat for half an hour drinking cappuccino and looking at the gorgeous view.

When she opened her box and saw what was inside, the store owner clapped her hands with joy and insisted on wearing her new hat back to the store. The shape accentuated her beautiful cheekbones, and the soft colors brought out the warmth of her skin.

When she walked away and looked back to wave, Kitty heard a man on the table beside her whistle softly under his breath. "Gorgeous." The words were just loud enough for Kitty to catch.

Kitty waved back at Annie.

"It looks beautiful on her."

Kitty looked up and saw Tom, the café owner, standing behind her, a tray in his hand. He nodded his respect at Kitty, then turned to his wife, who sat at a table close by with her twins. "Em, did you see Annie's new hat?"

Em, who ran the Beach Cove Bakery, nodded. "It really suits her so well. I wish I had something in that color." She hid a yawn behind her hand.

"I'm open for business," Kitty offered and smiled. Exhausted mothers were her specialty.

"I'll think about it." Em lifted her coffee cup. "As soon as I have a moment." She winked and took a sip.

"May I?" Tom pointed to the free chair next to Kitty.

Surprised, she gestured for him to sit. "Of course." Tom frequently talked to the patrons of his café, but he'd never yet asked Kitty whether he could join her at the table.

He put his tray on the table and took the bistro chair. "My mom said you and your sister inherited Martin's store and house."

"That's right," Kitty confirmed. "But if you're wondering what will happen to the candy store—we don't know yet. Neither of us feels a calling to continue running it, I'm afraid. Martin didn't ask us to, either. He just said to do what made us happy."

"Well...in fact, Em and I have been talking about it."

Kitty blinked. "About what?"

"Well, the candy store. I'm interested in making candy."

"My husband doesn't have enough going on with the café and the bakery," Em said. "He's already stretching hard candy in the kitchen at home. It's very good, Kitty."

"You two want to run the candy store?" Kitty angled her chair so she could also see Em.

"Very much." Tom rubbed a hand over his chin. "To be honest, I would make some changes. I'd like to set it up so people can watch us stretch and shape the candy in the window. Have you ever seen it done? It's fascinating."

"I'd like to boil sea salt taffy too," Em said while pushing the breakfast rolls out of her son's reach. "And we'd keep making his trademark candy apples, of course. He gave me the recipes years ago when I helped out in the summer."

"I had no idea, but it sounds interesting. It would be a pity to lose the store. Without wanting to give false hope, I like the idea. I will talk it over with my sister and get back to you."

"Good." Tom leaned back. "I thought maybe you wanted the store to sell hats."

"Maybe I still do." Kitty smiled. "But it would mean losing Martin's legacy. I understand you have a lot of tourists who are concerned."

"Oh man. Yes." Em sighed. "They're asking me a hundred times a day why it's closed. One of them even started crying when I told them we didn't know if it would open again."

"Uh-oh."

"Talk it over with Mela—we're just putting our interest in the store out there as an option." Em's fingers mechanically kneaded the last of her sesame bagel. As if she didn't notice what she was doing, the crumbs dropped on her lap and the floor where sparrows were already waiting. "Uh...Tom?"

"Yes." Tom inhaled and leaned forward again, the set of his shoulders tensing. "It'd be great if you could let us know."

"Is there anything else?" Kitty tilted her head. She could tell there was more.

Tom's neck, just above the collar of his white T-shirt, flushed a faint red. "We were wondering whether you have plans for Martin's house too."

"I'm afraid it's the same as for the store. At the moment, I'm staying with Mela, but I need a place of my own." Kitty loved her grandfather's house, and she needed a place to stay. Only days ago, she would have jumped at the opportunity. But things had changed in the last few days. "I feel at home in Bay Harbor, and of course, all my family is there."

Em hummed her agreement. "The cliff road between the towns is often closed due to bad weather. Sometimes you can't take it for weeks in the winter."

"She can always take the long road," Tom pointed out.

"How about I'll take that up with Mela too? Like I said, we haven't decided yet."

"Thank you." Tom rose and pushed the chair back. "Old fishing cottages don't come on the market very often. My family is quickly outgrowing our apartment." He nodded at the old brownstone building across the marketplace. "So far, we've put all our money into growing the café and the bakery. They're doing well now, so it's time to think about ourselves."

"We'd be happy to buy or rent." Em brushed the crumbs off her hands.

Kitty rose as well. "I have to go. Whether or not we decide not to use the buildings ourselves, you'll be the first to know."

Em wrestled a saltshaker from her protesting daughter. "We'll hire someone from Bay Harbor to help out in the candy store, if you like. Not to sound desperate, but we'll do *whatever* you want. Heck, it'll be a life of free coffee and cake for you and Mela both if you pick us." She grinned. "Shameless pitch. Real estate in Beach Cove is hard to get."

Kitty chuckled. "I understand. I'll call you soon." She shook the hand Tom extended.

"Let us know either way," he said and turned so his wife couldn't see his face. "And get me a date for a hat appointment," he whispered. "I want to surprise Em. Running a bakery and having twins isn't easy. She deserves a treat, and I saw the way she looked at Annie's hat."

"I'm wide open. Text me a time that's good."

"What are you two talking about?" Em called out.

Kitty smiled and waved, leaving Tom to explain.

She walked up cobbled Main Street, stopping by Sam's bookstore to say hi. Sam, claiming her books wanted her gone for the day, grabbed her hobo bag, slammed the door shut behind her, and joined Kitty. They went into the candy store across the street, dipping their hands in the glass jars to check the candy was still good, and then visited Martin's cottage to open the windows and air out the rooms.

Kitty told Sam about Tom and Em's interest in the buildings.

"It's perfect for them," Sam said after thinking about it. "The cottage is big enough that the twins will have their own rooms but not so big Em's will go crazy cleaning it. Obviously it's nice for them to be able to walk to work, and the kids will be able to bike to school."

"So your gut feeling is do it?" Kitty had heard enough about Sam's famed intuition to believe in it.

"My gut feeling is to outright sell them shop and store," Sam said. "Don't be shy asking for a fair price. Beach Cove real estate isn't cheap, and their stores do very well. I'm quite sure they'll offer over marketplace prices for everything the store and the cottage have to offer. Don't feel guilty. They really can afford it. If they would as much as blink in doubt, Ellie and Cate will start throwing fistfuls of money at you to make it happen. They're determined to keep their kids and the twins in Beach Cove. You can use the money to set yourself up nicely in Bay Harbor."

"I would like to stay in Bay Harbor." Kitty led the way into the little garden, where they watered the roses. "There's enough space here for a sandbox and a small swing set," she observed.

Unlike for herself, she had no problem thinking of the house for the young family. Suddenly, she was noticing all the ways it was perfect for them.

"Listen, Maisie and Ellie had their eye on a pretty little beach house in Bay Harbor for a while," Sam noted. "It became available just now, and they bought it half because they were charmed by it and half as an investment opportunity since Bay Harbor is picking up steam. It's a cute place. Quaint, and right on the beach. I mean, it's touching the sand." Sam turned off the patio faucet and rolled the hose into its copper pot.

"I didn't know," Kitty said.

Sam wiped her hands on her jeans. "It was in the works for a while. They spotted it on a walk and fell in love, so they asked their real estate agent to ferret out the owner. The owner wasn't willing to sell, but she was already elderly and actually passed away a few weeks before Martin did."

"Does it have a garden with roses?" Kitty wasn't really serious. But she did love Martin's roses.

"Not like these, but it has a yard full of wild beach roses," Sam offered. "Very pretty and maintenance-free. Of course you can always bring some of Martin's roses and put them in."

"Oh." As if a flip had been switched in her brain, suddenly there was nothing Kitty wanted more. She pressed together her lips to keep from jinxing it.

"There's not that many beach houses left even in Bay Harbor, and none as nice as this one, Maisie says. But." Sam paused significantly. "If you see your way to let Tom and Em have Martin's house here, Maisie and Ellie would be *ecstatic* to let you have the Bay Harbor beach house."

"They would?" Kitty opened the kitchen door, and they went back into the cottage. The kitchen had a breakfast nook that would be great for feeding the kids. Just the right height for two highchairs. Kitty turned away. The kitchen was cozy and small—but Tom and Em had chef kitchens at work. Maybe they wouldn't need much in their house.

Sam washed her hands in the sink and dried them on a dish towel that had a border of candy canes. "My feeling is that you would be happy in Bay Harbor. There's a cabin on the property that the former owner's husband used as a woodshop. It's stood untouched for a few years, but it's clean and dry and has electricity. Put a skylight into the roof, and you have the sweetest little studio for making hats."

Kitty laughed. "Stop! It sounds too good to be true. I'm scared it might not be real."

"I was wondering what the problem was! You should see your face." Sam chuckled. "I don't know why *I* want this so much—but I keep picturing the two of us having a glass of wine on the beach by your cabin, watching the waves. Maybe that's why." She grinned.

Kitty grinned back. "I really want that too. I'll talk to Mela. It's her house and store too."

"You do that." Sam knocked on the counter as if the house swap was already done. "If you sell the kids the candy store too, you'll have enough to give Mela her share and keep the beach house. Heck, you'll have enough left to take your time building the hat business."

"Seriously, stop." Kitty held her hands over her ears. "Things are never that easy. This is too much."

Sam reached out and pulled Kitty's hands down. "This is exactly right. It makes sense; everything would fall into place for so many people. Go talk to your sister."

Kitty, her heart beating with the radiant future Sam's words painted in her head, squared her shoulders. "If you let go of me, I will do it now."

Chapter 21

Mela tugged on her specially bought sand-colored linen dress. Then she fiddled with her hair, only dropping her hand to adjust her loosely knit cardigan. If this exhibition slash concert went well, the kids would be happy. And they would have a way of earning a livelihood that allowed them to stay in Bay Harbor.

A fisherman in a navy sweater and his wife nodded a greeting at Mela as they pushed past in the gathering crowd, and Mela nodded back. What were their names again? They were on the tip of her tongue.

"Everything's gorgeous," she whispered to Kitty. "I hope people like Sisley's paintings. Morris has had a lot of success with his music, but Sisley is putting herself out there for the first time. I'd buy all her paintings myself, but she wouldn't like it. Oh...I hope someone will buy one of her paintings."

"She's put in a lot of work. I'm sure it will go smoothly." Kitty didn't seem nervous at all. Maybe she knew something Mela didn't. Or maybe she wasn't nervous because it wasn't her kids' future careers and happiness that would be put to the test.

"Where are the books that used to be here?" Mela blinked as they crossed a beam of afternoon light falling through a window. "They haven't given them all away, have they?"

"A lot of them were donated, and Sam bought a bunch for the store. What's left is tucked away in the back rooms for now. Johanna has a plan for what to do with them. Donations and such."

"Ah. There's Morris's piano. It does look good! Transporting was such a drama. I hope he checked it's still tuned before he plays tonight."

Kitty chuckled. "Of course he has. He's playing all the time. I love hearing the music upstairs when I work."

"Of course," Mela echoed stupidly. She knew that. Morris couldn't stay away from his piano. He would be great. People always fell in love with him as soon as he started playing.

Kitty waved at another couple passing by.

Mela couldn't think of their names, either, but she recognized the appetizers Sunny and Amelie had brought over earlier. The woman ate a miniature quiche filled with mushrooms, cheese and herbs, and the husband had a mini Caprese salad served in a glass in one hand, a mini lobster mac and cheese tart in his other.

"Do you like it?" Kitty asked when they'd passed. "It looks great, doesn't it?"

"It's beautiful. Inviting." Mela hooked her arm under her sister's. "I thought we were early!" She lifted on tiptoes to see. "I almost wish there were fewer people. What did they put on the shelves behind the piano?"

"Let's go and check." They pushed through their neighbors and friends, waving and smiling. Most of Bay Harbor seemed to have come. Lobster fishers and trawler crews, their girlfriends and wives and kids, local restaurant and shop owners, and a lot of people Mela might've nodded and said hi to on a beach walk. Their faces looked familiar but so out of context in this venue Mela couldn't place them.

"Goodness, look at the buffet." Mela pointed as they passed the pushed-together library tables Sunny had covered with tablecloths purchased at Maison de Mer. Apparently, everyone was glad to have something to do in their sleepy small town.

"That's a good sign!" Not only had the locals turned out in full force. Unasked, they'd brought plates of cheese and bottles of wine, cookies, dips, chips, and anything else they thought should be part of the grand opening.

When they got closer to the piano, Kitty squinted. "Looks like Morris put vintage music scores for the piano on the shelves. Nice! Nice touch. And those are vinyl records of classic jazz. Blues, folk, and soul—that's all I can tell. Goodness, he's got a lot of them. And that over there is a bust of... I don't know."

"It's a college art project of no one in particular," Mela said. "I bought it for him when he was seven. He spotted it in a thrift store and liked it."

"Why not? It looks great." Kitty tugged on Mela's sleeve. "Let's go upstairs."

"Okay. The gallery. Exciting!" Eager to see what Sisley had done on her level, Mela turned on her heel, pulling her sister with her. Kitty laughed but matched Mela's speed as they wound their way back to the stairs. There were fewer people here. Mela hoped it was only because of the luscious buffet.

"Ooh. How pretty!" Mela breathed when the upstairs opened in front of them.

The intricate, vaulted ceiling of the library-turned-gallery, arching gracefully above the early viewers, was illuminated by the sunlight streaming through the octagonal window. It offered a breathtaking view of the sea to all who cared to look.

"My babies did this." Mela swallowed back rising tears. Nobody was surprised her kids were capable adults with talents and imagination—but to her, it was always amazing.

Kitty took her hand. "They did. They're wonderful, creative people, Mela. Be proud. *I'm* proud to the point of tears, and I'm only half an aunt who made their acquaintance barely six months ago."

"And look at those paintings. Please explain to me how she didn't make it through college..." The wall had been painted a warm and inviting white, and last Mela had been up here, it had been a cheerful, bright, open, and empty hall. Now, Sisley's large art pieces dotted the walls. Colorful and large, the paintings transformed the space.

"It's getting fuller and fuller," Kitty murmured. "I know for a fact the family over there lives in Sandville. These aren't only people from Bay Harbor, Mela."

"I suppose word spread." Mela too knew the Sandville family—they owned the supermarket that was under construction there. The couple chatting with them was from Beach Cove. And unless Mela was mistaken, the little old lady wearing huge sunglasses and standing very close to the most colorful abstract was none other than Mrs. Piper, the owner of the Bay Port department store.

"Let's get a look at the art before more people come upstairs," Mela said. "I haven't seen everything Sisley's painted since she moved out."

"I haven't seen all of it either. The important thing is that she's productive." Kitty sounded satisfied. "It means she loves doing what she's doing."

"Well." Mela cleared the wobble that was part worry part pride from her throat. "If only she can find someone to buy a painting tonight. Just as a sign that she can pull it off. I think it would boost her confidence." Of her three children, Sisley had always been the one to doubt herself.

Kitty pushed her hair back, the gesture almost impatient. "She's got Bennett to fall back on, at least until she's found her niche. Sometimes it takes a while for an artist to start selling. She'll be okay as long as she keeps going."

"I want a closer look." Mela nodded hello at a man eating and sidestepped more people before they finally reached paintings.

Mela inhaled and focused on the art. "Oh. This is...completely different."

Beside her, Kitty hummed. "I've seen this one; it's one of my favorites. What do you think? Do you like it?"

Mela came even closer and lifted her hand halfway, her fingers longing for the shades of blue and purple, the glittering accent lines of silver and gold that danced around the canvas like a school of fish.

"Don't touch." Kitty chuckled and pressed Mela's hand down. "Do you like it?"

"I love it," Mela said, sounding helpless. "I'm so glad I love it." How had Sisley managed a technique like this?

"Were you afraid you wouldn't?"

"No." Mela smiled back. "But it's always a relief when it's so good you're actually surprised, isn't it? To be honest...I'm not only surprised, I'm dumbfounded. I expected something good. But this—it's *really* good."

"She titled it *Below the sea*." Kitty pointed at the label.

Mela would have liked to spend more time to study the label and admire the painting. But another group was shuffling closer, as hesitant to interrupt as they were eager to see.

"Let's keep moving." They went to the next one. "*Sea Meadow*," Mela read. "Oh. Sea meadow. Interesting." Painted in vibrant shades, the sea was a mix of crashing waves and rolling tides. It had a distinctly different feel than the last painting. Mela tilted her head. "This wouldn't have something to do with Finn's beach, would it?"

Finn's beach was infamously dangerous—one of Beach Cove's wild underwater currents rushed the tide faster over the beach than people could get back to the stairs leading up the cliff and to safety. Over the years, many tourists had to be saved by local fishermen before the town closed the beach.

"You're right. Like you're standing on the meadow to the side, looking down on it."

"I don't know about this one. It's so...evocative." Mela shook herself. She remembered only too well standing there while the police were searching for her mother's remains. "Too much for me. What's next?"

They moved from one painting to the next, pushed and pulled by the crowd, to admire the art. Bold, fiery oranges and reds that weaved together to create the illusion of sunlight reflecting off the ocean's surface, deep blues and greens mixed with bright yellows, swirling in mesmerizing patterns, blues, greens, and purples depicting the powerful yet peaceful movement of the waves.

"What do you think?" Sisley, holding a glass of prosecco, appeared in front of them. Bennett towered over her like a bodyguard. Lovie was sleeping in his arms, her curls sweaty from the heat in the room.

Mela took her daughter's free hand. "They are unbelievable. I don't know what to say, sweetheart. I expected them to be good, but they're unbelievable."

"Thank you!" Sisley beamed and turned to look at Bennett. He smiled, looking almost as proud as Mela felt.

A sudden arpeggio pealed up the stairs, its drama followed by a simple melody as beautiful as a morning by the sea.

"Morris is playing!" Sisley sounded excited. "Mom, do you like it?"

"Uh." Mela swallowed again, but this time, it didn't do the trick. She sniffled. "Um."

Sisley laughed and pressed a kiss on Mela's cheek. "I love you, Mom. None of this would have happened without you. Should we go down to see Morris play? If we fit. I have no idea where all the people come from."

Mela took the tissue Kitty was handing her. "Sure. I'd love—"

"*Excuse* me." The little old lady with the sunglasses—possibly Mrs. Piper—pushed between them.

Chapter 22

Mrs. Piper removed her large glasses, stowing them in the black Dior bag dangling from her forearm. "I'd like to purchase a couple of the paintings. You are the artist?"

"I am." Sisley held out her hand, but Mrs. Piper ignored it.

Mela had heard rumors that the grand dame of Bay Port was cotton dry—but she also heard how angry she had been at what happened to Kitty and Johanna.

"There are no prices noted." Mrs. Piper narrowed her eyes and sized Sisley up as if she were for sale herself. "I'd like to know how much you want for—" She consulted her phone. "*Sea Meadow*, *Waves of Contrast*, and *Lighthouse in Moonlight*."

Mela saw her daughter's throat move. Sisley had never sold a painting before. Mela held her breath, crossing her fingers that this would end well.

"Five each," Bennett said firmly. From the look Sisley gave her fiancé, Mela knew Sisley had meant to ask for less. Sisley had explained that at first, she'd have to sell at a loss, just to get word out about her work. Three hundred, maybe.

"Five? Hmm." Mrs. Piper turned to look at the paintings again. "Half the game is provenance, isn't it?"

"What do you mean, provenance?" Bennett asked.

"Well, it's all about who owned the piece of art before." Mrs. Piper said over her shoulder. "If Marilyn Monroe owned it, people will pay more for it. Obviously."

"I see." Lovie stirred, and Bennett rocked her. "Well, everything here is being sold for the first time. But the price is firm."

Sisley's chest expanded to speak, but Kitty held up a finger behind Mrs. Piper, warning her niece to stay quiet. Slowly, Sisley released the breath again.

"Well... Hmm."

Sisley blinked. "No, he's just kidding. I—"

"Ah! No." Mrs. Piper turned back and held up a hand. "Don't, please. He already said five."

"But I—"

"Tut! I'm keen on supporting young artists, and I'm an avid collector. If you sell them to me for five each, right now, it will create a bit of a stir for you. Other collectors watch closely what I do. You'll get the price you already asked—plus invaluable PR."

"I could use a stir," Sisley said meekly.

Relieved, Mela let out an internal sigh. Sisley would give away paintings for free to create a buzz.

"Smart decision. Well, I'll take *Waves of Contrast* and *Lighthouse in Moonlight*, five each." Mrs. Piper turned back. She weaved her head. "Oh, and I might as well take *Meadow* before someone else comes along. Though it's not quite as expressive as the other two." She glanced at Sisley. "What do you say? Deal?"

"Deal," Sisley said before anyone else could. "Thank you."

Kitty leaned forward. "And you are...?"

"Mrs. Therese Piper. Are you her agent?"

"Sisley represents herself."

"She does?"

"I'm Kitty Sullivan. We were in touch about the—"

"Yes. Yes. Of course." A faint glow colored the old lady's pale cheeks, and she waved the air as if it was hot. "Not here, please. I promise I'm taking care of it."

"I know."

"Oh. Good." Mrs. Piper turned to Sisley. "Is a check okay?"

"Sure," Sisley said. "Would you like to go use the desk over there?"

"Not necessary." Mrs. Piper opened her Dior purse and pulled out a rather ratty checkbook, expertly flipping it open and quickly scribbling in it with a slim silver pen. She ripped off the check and handed it to Sisley.

Sisley's eyes widened. "Hang on, you made a mistake."

Mrs. Piper's elegant eyebrows crumpled. "I'm excellent at math. We said *Waves*, *Lighthouse* and *Meadow*." She craned her neck to look at the number she'd written. "What's the problem?"

"But..." Sisley pointed. "You wrote the check out to fifteen *thousand*." Sisley cleared her throat. "That would be quite the surprise for you when I cash it."

Mrs. Piper stared at Sisley, then at the check. Suddenly her thin lips curved into a smile. "Dear child, do you mean to say I could have had the paintings for five *hundred* each?"

Sisley nodded.

Bennett closed his eyes.

Sisley held out the check. "Here. I didn't mean to trick you."

Mela's eyes went between her daughter, the old lady, and Bennett as if they were playing a complicated game of ping-pong.

Mrs. Piper took the check. "I'm...well. I never." She shook her head as if she was dazed. Then she folded the check and opened her purse.

Kitty pursed her lips to let out a tense breath. Like Mela, her gaze bounced between the players. "I say you are worth more than a few hundred, Sisley, honey. I'm not a collector, but *I'd* pay more than that. A lot more."

Lovie stirred, and her rosebud mouth opened in a disoriented whimper.

Mrs. Piper's Dior snapped shut with a click. "This one is on me." She held out the check. "Since I know your esteemed family..." She cleared her throat twice. "I stick to my offer. And let me tell you—for the next one, start at eight. Thousand. Not hundred. Don't go below six. You *are* worth it."

"Oh. OH." Sisley's eyes widened.

The corner of Mrs. Piper's mouth lifted as she took Sisley's hand and closed her fingers over the slip of paper.

"Sure?" Sisley sounded as disoriented as her baby.

Mrs. Piper patted her hand once and then stepped back. "You're not going to be a secret for long. It doesn't happen often, but I've seen it before. Promise to keep at it."

Sisley's hand trembled as it sank to her side. "But are you sure?"

The thin shoulders in the vintage Chanel shrugged. "I can't eat my money, can I? And I have no heirs to get mad if I make a mistake. Not that it would be any of their business... Either way, I bought something pretty to look at." She stuffed her checkbook back and glanced at Kitty. "My personal assets are, of course, legally separate from those of Piper Department Store."

"Good gracious," Kitty said. "I already told you we're not going to sue. Please do not worry about it."

"Hmm." The thin upper lip moved. "Maybe you and I can have a gin and tonic together sometime."

"Sure. I suppose."

Mrs. Piper nodded, satisfied the peace was real. "By the way, are you the one who's the hatter?"

Kitty's head tilted in acknowledgment. "Yup."

"I'd like to order a few hats for myself. But first, we drink together."

"Okay."

There was a short pause. Then, "And you are?" Mrs. Piper squinted at Mela.

"Sisley's mother, Pamela."

"Ah, the politician's ex-wife. Yes?"

Mela felt her eyebrows crawl upward to meet her bangs. "Yes."

"Very good. I'm glad you managed to get yourself back to the coast. Well, I'll have someone pick up the paintings, then."

"Right now?"

A slightly pained expression at Sisley's naivete lowered Mrs. Piper's eyelids. "No, not now. Once your exhibition is over." She held out a hand to Mela, Mela shook, not quite knowing why she'd been the one offered the honor, and then Mrs. Piper lifted her phone to her ear and pushed her way toward the staircase, disappearing in the crowd.

They stared after her.

"Do I wrap the paintings?" Sisley handed Kitty her prosecco as if she needed her hands free to start packing up. "Bubble wrap? What?"

Kitty handed the glass back. "You don't have to do it yet, anyway," she said. "You're practically famous now, kid. I wouldn't put it past that lady to make it happen."

Mela waved at one of the hired local teens who had started to offer trays of appetizers and drinks around. "Congratulations, baby. I'd say you're off to a marvelous start."

The teen arrived, and everyone took a filled flute.

"No more worrying that the cost of the prosecco is covered," Bennett said. They laughed, their relief palpable, and clinked their glasses to another dizzying arpeggio drifting upstairs.

"Are you already selling?" A rotund man shoved himself into the circle. "I didn't know, I thought... What about *Waves of Contrast*?"

Sisley lowered her glass. "I'm sorry, it just sold."

The man's bottom lip dropped in frustration. "What was the bid?"

Kitty tilted her head. "What would you have offered?"

"I would've... I wished there was a way to know when people start selling." He pulled out a handkerchief to wipe his glistening temples. "Piper, was it?"

"Maybe," Kitty said before Sisley could. "Maybe not. For privacy reasons, we—"

He grimaced. "It's always Piper." He stuffed the tissue back into his suit jacket. "What else did she buy?"

"Which ones are you interested in?" Sisley asked back.

"*Lighthouse*. And *Meadow*. Maybe *Seabird*."

"*Lighthouse* and *Meadow* sold too. But *Seabird* is available and so is *Driftwood Blues*." She smiled. "*Driftwood* is my favorite."

"What did Piper offer?" He hesitated. "Eight thousand each?"

"I really can't talk about it." Sisley shrugged her regrets. Another person was approaching their group and she smiled a greeting.

The man moved to block the new person. "She offered more, did she? Fine. Ten. Ten thousand each. Last offer. I better just take them before someone else hears Piper is snatching you up. Is a check all right? I'm Gale Henderson, president of North East Electric. I'm good for it."

"Nice to meet you, Mr. Henderson. A check is fine." Sisley changed her glass to the other hand and wiped her fingers on her sky-blue linen dress. Maybe they were greasy from a mini quiche. More likely she was sweating with nerves despite her newfound confidence. "Thank you."

Lovie threw herself backward like a seal, and Bennett caught her. "I'm going to change Lovie's diaper," he said shakily.

"Great." Sisley winked at him.

He shook his head at her, a smile on his lips.

"I still have the diaper bag in my studio," Kitty said. "Come with me. The bathroom's going to be crowded."

The president handed Sisley his check. "I'll have someone pick them up in a couple of weeks, then," he said. "If you don't mind sending the paperwork with it."

Sisley shifted her weight on the other foot. "Paperwork as in...?"

"The bill of sale. An invoice stating copyright and reproduction rights and all that. Uh...do you have an agent?"

"Yes." Mela slipped her arm under Sisley's. "She practically does."

His eyes went between mother and daughter. "Well, your agent knows what to do." He shook hands with Sisley and left.

"My knees are going to give out," Sisley murmured. "My palms are slippery with sweat."

"Are you talking sales over here?" The blocked person had disappeared, but a couple eagerly took the president's spot. "Is *Waves of Contrast* for sale?"

"No, it sold." Sisley said weakly. "I won't do any more sales today. I'll give you a call tomorrow if you have a card."

The woman's face fell, and the man put his arm around her shoulder. "What did it go for? Maybe I can make a better offer."

"Thank you." Sisley swayed, but Mela steadied her. "But it really is taken. I'll have another exhibition soon."

"My wife liked *Waves* if you can make another one like it." He let go of the woman and pulled out his phone. "When is your next exhibition scheduled, please?"

Mela felt Sisley shake. With laughter or fear, she couldn't tell.

"I have no idea. When I've had time to paint more?"

He let his phone sink and patted his pockets. "Here." He handed her a card. "I'm interested in your vernissage."

Sisley cleared her throat. "My what?"

"Your vernissage. Your preview. The showing before the exhibition. I'd like to get an invitation if you wouldn't mind." The arm went back over his partner's shoulders, who smiled bravely.

"I love what you do," the woman said. "We own a cruise business, and you should think I'd get to spend more time at sea. But mostly I work from an office in Boston. I'm forever looking for pieces that remind me of the coast in Maine. My parents retired to Seal Harbor; that's how we heard about this town. What I'm trying to say is, we're around. And we're interested in adding you to our collection. My mom will want a look, too."

"Do let me know." Her husband pointed at his card.

"I will. Thank you." Sisley breathed the words more than she said them.

The couple left. "I think I'm going to be sick." Sisley pressed a hand to her stomach. "I don't feel so good."

Mela squeezed her daughter's hand. "You're doing amazing. Try to hold on. We'll freak out together after everyone has left."

Sisley drained her glass. She was pale, but a flush was emerging from her flowy hippie dress. "Promise?" she asked and lifted another flute from a passing tray.

Mela took it from her and returned it to another tray. "Promise. Congrats, honey. You remember Sam's husband, David, don't you? He paints. I saw Sam earlier, so David must be here too. We'd better find them and ask whether he will share his agent."

"An agent," Sisley repeated mechanically.

"Oh you poor baby. Usually I'd say don't worry, but..."

Sisley's eyes widened as if Mela were going to drop the shoe she was waiting for. "But what, Mom?"

Mela smiled. "But the local art scene is officially in love with you. You're in for a ride."

Chapter 23

The mid-morning sky shimmered a soft, hazy gray. Scattered wisps of cloud floated in the air like warm, languid feathers.

Kitty got out of the car. The street ended in a small semicircle that would park two big or three small cars. To the left, a boardwalk led into the dunes toward the sea. To the right was a grove of feathery beach pines.

"How did Maisie and Ellie even find this?" Mela shook her head. "I live here, and I didn't know there was a house here."

"Everyone automatically turns toward the boardwalk," Kitty pointed out. "The house is on the other side."

"I thought there was a path?" Mela pointed at the pines.

Kitty took off her knit sweater and tossed it in the car. It was too warm. "Maisie said the heather grew over it. Let's go find it and look at the house while we are waiting for them."

"Maisie's never late. Ellie, maybe. But Maisie?"

"The rain last night flooded the cliff road. She had to turn back and take the long way around."

"I didn't notice any rain... Was it one of those Beach Cove weather things?"

"I suppose." Beach Cove had its own microclimate. Why, Kitty had no idea. The cliff was high, but it wasn't exactly a mountain.

They crossed the small parking lot. "There's the path." Mela pushed the heather aside with her sandal. "Huh. So tucked away."

"I don't think a lot of tourists will see this."

"There's no way. Like you say, the boardwalk draws all the attention."

Kitty stepped on the soft pine needle carpet, following the faint trace of the hidden path. One of the wispy clouds shifted. The sun filtered through the pine needles, casting dappled shadows on the path. "It smells good." She drew in as much air as she could, closing her eyes to savor the smell of salt in the air mixed with the sweet scent of the pines. "Gah, I wish I could bottle this. Better than a heady perfume."

"I've always liked heather," Mela said at the same time as Kitty said, "I like the purple." They laughed.

Mela leaned to inspect a bush. "Huckleberries. Too early for them, but you can make jam in August. There are probably blueberries in there too. We should see if we can pick some for the kids. Finn sometimes made blueberry pancakes for us. I forgot about that."

Kitty smiled. "I'm glad he found Julie." She stepped over a gnarly root. "I'm glad he found happiness."

"It must've been difficult. Martin said he loved us both, but he couldn't get you and he couldn't acknowledge me."

"I'm glad times are different now."

"Me too. Oh, ouch." Mela's ankle had hit a root.

"Careful." Kitty waited for her sister and pointed out the next root peeping through the pine bedding.

"They're like creaky floorboards; we'll just have to remember where they are."

"Listen, I really appreciate you helping me out like this." Kitty saw the pine boughs lighten. She turned to Mela. The parking lot was gone from view.

"Helping you out how? If you're referring to the money from the inheritance, I'm not doing you any favors since you won't let me."

After talking numbers with their Beach Covian friends, they'd found that Kitty's half of the money was more than enough to buy

Maisie's Bay Harbor cottage. Plus, there was enough left over to last Kitty while she set up shop—plenty for a year or two, more if she was frugal. All she had to worry about was tax and food and utilities.

They stepped out of the shade of the trees and onto the sand.

"It is literally built on the beach?" Mela shook her head. "I don't know about that... Remember Sunny's landslide?"

"Oh. Oh." Kitty had spotted the house—a cozy, shingled cottage nestled in the dunes, with a wraparound porch looking out at the ocean in the front and a wild little garden in the back. The windows were big, with white and blue shutters that would keep her safe from storms.

This must be love at first sight, Kitty thought. For her, it had happened with a house, not a man. "Look at the flowers," she said helplessly.

"Beautiful. I like even better that it's not sitting on shifting sand after all. Looks like it's built on an outcropping of bedrock. There wouldn't be any grass otherwise."

"I don't care what it's built on."

Mela took Kitty's hand and pulled her over the sand toward the cottage. "Such a sweet mix of forest and beach. Whoever built this was smart."

"Whoever built this was in love." Kitty stopped by the gate of the faded picket fence to admire the speckled petals of the wild foxglove that swayed in the ocean breeze. There were delicate white daisies, their yellow middles glowing. Tall lupines covered the distance to the pines in shades of purple and blue. To Kitty's delight, pale pink beach roses intertwined with bright-green raspberries and yellow buttercups that seemed to sparkle in the morning sun.

Mela whistled softly. "You'll have your work cut out cleaning this mess up."

Kitty pushed her hands on her hips. "It's perfect as is. Nobody touches a thing."

To her surprise, Mela burst out laughing. "I'm just teasing you. You're dead gone, aren't you?"

"Have you ever seen anything this perfect?"

"It is a bit ramshackle." Mela held up a hand before Kitty could say anything. "Hush. It needs some fixing up."

"But I—"

"I've helped renovate the motel. I have an eye for this. The plumbing's going to—"

"I already made a list," Maisie's voice came from behind them, and they wheeled around. She waved.

"Maisie!" Mela held out her hands, and Maisie grasped them to say hello.

"I braved the cliff road after all." She pushed back her silver hair. "Hello, you two. Would you like to go in?"

"Yes," Mela said. Kitty only nodded—she wanted to go in, but she also wanted to stay out here.

Maisie handed her a key. "Ellie and I are glad you're considering swapping Martin's place for this. Houses like his don't come on the market anymore—they're handed on inside families from generation to generation. At least in Beach Cove."

"I like the porch," Kitty said stupidly. It was almost too much to think this should be hers. She'd sit here with family and visitors, watching the sea, thinking about her hats, growing old. The sea breeze took care of bugs and the roof of rain. In the mornings, she'd be out here drinking coffee while—

"If it wasn't there already, you'd have to build it," Maisie agreed and took the key back. "I have to hustle along; we have new visitors coming to the inn." She opened the gate and marched toward the cottage, taking the two stairs to the porch.

Mela pulled Kitty along; Kitty had just enough sense to reach for a foxglove. Her fingertips touched a velvety leaf in passing and set the tall plant dancing. A bumble bee buzzed its protest, backing out of the flower. "I looove bumblebees," Kitty murmured.

Her sister and her friend laughed. "I think Kitty likes it!" Maisie turned the key in the door. "Here. Come have a look inside. It's bigger than it looks."

There was little talking as they walked through the house. Kitty would have taken it gutted, but there was no need for compromise. She loved the inside at first glance too even though the porch and the flowers would always win.

As it was, the door opened into a cheerful kitchen, beach-themed with shining white cabinets and vibrant accents of ocean blue. A rustic farmhouse table with benches occupied the place under the sea view window while the sink looked out at the wild garden. A small center island was perfect for cooking up delicious dishes or sharing a cup of tea.

"It's big." Mela looked around, appraising everything as if backing out was still an option.

"The lady who owned it liked to cook, and Ellie had Tom upgrade the appliances a little. It's all modern; it all works. This is the living room." Maisie waved them on.

Kitty went into the living room with shabby-chic white-washed furniture and a large window front to take in the views of the beach. A cozy sofa and armchairs with vintage-style patterned pillows and pastel-colored curtains were grouped around a fireplace that housed a large pellet stove.

"Very low heating cost in the winter," Maisie remarked. "We put that in too. Open fireplaces can be difficult when it's windy outside. And this close to the sea, it'll be windy. Did you see this is a door? You can open it and practically be part of the beach."

Kitty noticed her sister glance at her. She cleared her throat. "I like it." She picked up a fluffy pillow and set it down again. Sitting here in the winter, cozy-warm, looking out at the icy sea would be…and of course in the summer, she could open the door leading out on the porch.

"Here's the bathroom. It's the only one, I'm afraid, but it's a decent size."

Kitty peeked at the bathroom with a claw-foot tub on a cheerful mosaic-tile floor, a nautical-inspired mirror, and a shower door with a ceramic octopus for a handle. A small chandelier hung from the ceiling right over the bathtub.

She still had those bath salts sitting in the roof apartment. She could use them here. Though now she was rich, she could buy fancy fizzing bath salt balls, lock herself in here, and never come out again.

"No worries," Mela whispered beside her. "You can always put up guests at my house or at the motel if you don't want to share your space."

Kitty wasn't the type to invite guests she didn't want to share her bathroom with. In all honesty, though, she couldn't see herself sharing this house. Day guests, sure. But at night, this was her place, to curl up and dream.

"Hey," Mela said.

Kitty startled and turned to her. "What?"

"Did you hear what I said?"

Kitty squinted at her. "Depends. What did you say?"

"Okay, she's a goner," Mela told Maisie. "I was going to play it cool, but she clearly *likes* this house."

"Well, let's look at the rest anyway. There's a direct door to the bedroom behind the shower." Maisie crossed the bathroom and opened another white door.

Kitty followed obediently. The room had a four-poster bed draped in light muslin curtains and a quilt made of bright, patterned fabrics. Bright, airy curtains billowed in the ocean breeze, and outside swayed the sweet-smelling sea of lupines.

"We accidentally left the window open. Sorry about that." Maisie strode to the window and closed it. "There's a couple of big linen closets you can access from the corridor outside and a small pantry off the kitchen I forgot to show you. The only thing missing is a mudroom, but you can make do with the big porch. Come on out. I'll show you the cabin you can use as a studio. There's still woodworking stuff in there, but Gordy is going to clear it out this weekend, and then we'll have our cleaners take care of it. It'll be sparkling clean when you move in. Also, before I forget, Em hired a master gardener to take a few of Martin's roses and plant them here."

"Where?" Kitty still felt like this was all a dream. It blanketed her thoughts and made it hard to talk. Fuzzy thoughts interrupted the direct line from her brain to her lips.

Maisie smiled. "Wherever you like." Mela made a sound as if she was trying not to laugh, and even Maisie cleared her throat. "Well—what do you think? Good enough to swap us Martin's house in Beach Cove? I know the price doesn't match, but we'll pay the difference cash."

Kitty turned. "Mela?"

Mela shook her head. "I don't need another house, neither here nor in Beach Cove. This one's all you. If you want this cottage instead of Martin's house, say yes now."

"Yes," Kitty said, feeling her lungs expand. "Yes please." Suddenly, a rock tumbled off her vocal cords as she realized that this *was* true. This was her house at the beach. She'd live here until they carried her out feet first because there was no other way she'd ever leave this place again. "I love this house. I love everything about it. I can see myself living here and working here and having my friends and family over. There are so many things I already want to do—not fix things; they're perfect. But things like reading a book or putting my feet up by the fire, look out at the sea every morning and watch the light wash over the pines in the evening. I want to listen to the gulls crying and pick lupines and foxglove for kitchen bouquets—"

"Foxglove is toxic," Mela interrupted her and took her by the elbow. "Don't put it on the kitchen table at least. All right, Maisie, no need to pretend this isn't working out great for Kitty. What do we do next?"

Maisie hooked her arm under Kitty's other arm. "We call Em and let her know. Her raspberry rolls this morning turned out terrible. She can't focus. She's as madly in love with Martin's house as Kitty is with this one."

They went into the kitchen, where they had electricity, gas, water, and tea bags, and brewed a pot while putting Em and Tom on Maisie's speaker so they all could share in the joy of the good news.

"When can I move in?" Kitty asked when they stepped back into the shoes they'd left on the porch.

Maisie handed her the key. "Today, if you like. Ellie must have had the utilities connected, so you're all set. You can change the names on the accounts after we have settled the paperwork. It'll be easier to wait."

Kitty took the key, feeling the cool metal press into her palm. "What about all the furniture and the...well, everything? The previous owner still has her plates and teapots and tea bags and linen here."

"Her son said it all came with the house if we wanted. We wanted, and he was glad not to have to pay for cleaning it out. He lives in South Carolina, you know. His mother's old teapots in Maine were a bit of a problem. Now you can have them."

They walked back to where they'd parked side by side. Maisie's cell phone rang, and she glanced at it. "I gotta go." She tucked the phone away again. "My lawyer has the paperwork ready. Do we have a deal?" She held out her hand.

Mela shook, and so did Kitty. Maisie hugged them and hurried off, managing to make the tires of her old Acura squeal as she peeled out of the tiny parking lot.

"You know," Mela said after the sound from the engine had once again given place to the background music of screaming gulls and waves crashing on rocks, "I'm starting to suspect there's more to Maisie's guests than we know. Don't you?"

Kitty was too happy to contradict her sister. "Definitely." Her phone vibrated in the pocket of her jeans. She pulled it out and checked the message. "Oh!"

"Anything important?"

"The younger Mrs. Botrel." Kitty put a hand to her head. "She won the lottery."

"Like, how?" Mela opened the door and gestured Kitty inside.

"No, she's actually won the lottery. At least that's what she says." Kitty folded herself into Mela's car.

Mela closed her door and let the motor rumble to life. "How much did she win?"

Kitty put her seatbelt on. "Not a million, she writes. But more than a half." Another text pinged on her phone. "Enough to keep the store a while longer. And..." Kitty laughed as another text popped up. "She says it's because of the hat I made her. The owner of the Sandville Deli liked it so much she offered Annie a lottery ticket in exchange for my number. Well—how about that? I'm glad for her."

Another text dinged. "Oh! The Starfish report is going to mention me in the article about Annie's win. Annie wants to know if that's okay."

"Say yes." Mela smiled. "Maybe you'll have more business coming your way too." She turned onto a bigger road, and soon, they were driving on Main Street. "I'm so happy for Annie. She put her all into the Bay Harbor store, and we certainly need it. If they can hang on just a little longer, Bay Harbor will attract the crowd to make it work for her."

"It's surprising how hanging in a little longer has a way of fixing things, isn't it?" Kitty said. "Let's see what happens next. For once, I can't wait to see what it is."

Chapter 24

Mela opened the door for her aunt. Sunny's new hip worked better than she'd hoped, but Mela's car sat low to the ground.

"I can do it!" Sunny heaved herself out of the seat and stood. "Oof. Thank you, honey."

"You're welcome." Mela closed the door and slipped her arm under her aunt's. "Ready?"

"I couldn't tell you." Sunny chuckled. "A bakery is something else, isn't it?"

"It sure is." Mela paused to take in the sight. Busy with her honeybees and the art event, the motel, and the last preparations for the wedding, she'd not had time to stop by the mill for a while.

Today was the big reveal. The construction team tasked with rebuilding had left, a cleaning team had washed the dust off the walls and floors, and Peter and Charlie were ready to show the bakery to Sunny.

Peter, especially.

Mela knew he wanted the two of them to live in a house by themselves—but she knew that even more, he wanted to make Sunny just as happy as he could.

"Take a deep breath." Mela had parked so Sunny couldn't see the mill yet. "Ready?"

"I've seen the mill before," Sunny said patiently.

"Yes, but that was years and years ago. You haven't come here since the landslide, have you?"

"No. I couldn't walk. Besides, it wasn't a place to come and visit since it was privately owned."

"It's still privately owned." Mela led Sunny around the car. "Only now it's ours. Okay—open your eyes."

Sunny's eyes flew open. For a while, she only looked. Then she put her other hand on Mela's arm as well. "Oh. Oh, my heart," she murmured. "That does look pretty, doesn't it?"

"Yes. It does." The mill sat by a creek that wound its way through the meadows before feeding into a cranberry bog.

Peter had insisted on putting in a big bluestone terrace where Sunny could sit and enjoy the sun. It looked out at the cranberry bog that was a short mile away on even ground, perfect for a constitutional walk. Another mile, and the bog changed into wide tidal flats framed by ancient cypresses on either side. Right now, the sea filled the flats, and they glistened bright blue under the spotless afternoon sky. But even when the tide was low and the flats drained, it was a view that should be an oil painting hanging in a museum.

Sunny made no attempt at walking on, so Mela stood with her, giving her time to soak in the setting. "Take your time. You only get one first impression, so you might as well enjoy it."

She held her face in the sun. Even from there, she could hear the soft squawking of the gulls that followed the fish trawlers and lobster boats. But there were also the more melodic sounds of blackbirds and robins singing in the grass. In the mornings and evenings, when the sky bathed in red and gold, Mela had heard the silver-fluted song of the hermit thrush that lived in one of the defunct wings of the mill.

"It smells so good," Sunny said suddenly. "What is that?"

Mela inhaled. "It's the scent of fresh hay, I'd say." She opened her eyes and smiled. "It always smells sweeter when you don't have to cut it yourself, don't you think?"

"I can smell the bog."

"Oh. That too." Most cranberry bogs, like this one, were artificial, made to grow and harvest the tart red berries. They didn't smell of sour peat but had the tangy, sweet smell of cranberry. "You'll be able to watch them harvest berries while you sit out here drinking coffee and eating croissants with marmalade and jam."

"You too." Sunny patted Mela's arm. "Now I want to see the mill. The view is pretty enough to make me feel like I'm floating a foot off the ground. I think it will do me good to worry about rotting wood crumbling into my coffee cake batter."

Mela smiled but didn't reply. They started walking up a crunchy gravel path that led from the parking area to a few flat stone steps. "Look up." Mela stopped below the wings. They looked small from a distance but not this close. "It's huge."

They put their heads into their necks and squinted up the majestic construction. The tip of the mill reached high into the sky, and the old wings looked too heavy for any wind to move them. Mela hoped they were fixed in position for the sake of the hermit thrush nesting in the spokes.

The door on top of the steps opened. "Welcome!" Peter stood on the stone threshold. He was wearing his work clothes, old jeans splattered with paint and motor oil and whatever else he'd worked on that didn't wash out, and a T-shirt. He ran a hand through his hair, then kissed Mela on the lips and Sunny on the cheek. "I've been waiting for you." He sounded like a boy waiting for Christmas to start.

"Let's have a look then," Sunny said good-humoredly. "See what you did to that bakery of yours."

"Come on in."

They stepped inside. In passing, Mela asked, "Is Charlie here as well?"

"He went on a walk with Amelie," Peter replied. "They should be back soon. Amelie wanted to pick some wildflowers for the tables."

"Goodness," Sunny said softly. "Will you look at that? Here I thought it'd be broken boards and bricks on the ground."

"Oh no." Peter let the heavy door fall shut. "It's all done. Well, almost all done. We're still waiting for some of the kitchen equipment. But this is just the entrance room."

They were in a small room with a stone floor polished to a soft gleam from years of feet walking in and out. A couple of chairs and a small table stood to the left. On the wall to the right hung framed landscapes as well as an old-fashioned brass coat rack for visitors, with matching brass umbrella stands framing the door.

"Can't have wet umbrellas around when you grind flour. Come through here, you two." Peter opened the next door. It led into an open room full of light, with white-washed walls, exposed wooden beams, and a gleaming counter of more polished brass. A large front window overlooked the creek, with the bog and the ocean stretching out beyond. On the far side was a gigantic fireplace with a simple screen to keep embers inside. In the middle of the room lay a round millstone, and scattered throughout stood wooden bistro sets, their tables decorated with small white vases.

Sunny shook her head. "You have space for people to sit?"

Peter nodded. "The kitchen door is behind the counter. Let me show you."

"Ah. I might have to sit down and look for a moment. An old woman isn't an express train."

Peter chuckled. "Do you want a coffee? We have a behemoth of a coffee maker. Tom said it was the best, so Charlie had it sent from Italy without asking another question."

"How am I going to know what buttons to press on a behemoth of a coffee maker from Italy?" Sunny's voice wavered. "Are there levers?"

"We hire someone to do it for you," Peter said calmly. "You can't bake and do the counter. You'll never have to touch the coffee machine if you don't want to."

There was a small pause. "But I want to," Sunny said finally. "I can do it."

"Sunny." Mela took her aunt's hands. "This bakery is going to be proper work. But there will be staff. All you're supposed to do is test out new recipes and show your bakers how to make them."

"I know it looks grand." Peter looked worried as he crossed his arms in front of his chest. "But that's Charlie. He wanted Bay Harbor to have a place where the senior club can play canasta and drink coffee in peace and quiet and, well...he's all for going big or going home."

"There's the Beach Bistro," Mela pointed out. "It's where the seniors always meet."

"Now that the motel is full and the Beach Cove tourists can come over the cliff to visit, the Beach Bistro is overwhelmed. They can't just push half their tables together anymore so the seniors can sit together. Besides, it closes in winter. It's just too expensive to heat the Bistro when the freezing winds come in from the open sea. That entire beach turns into an icicle."

"That's true." Sunny knocked a knuckle on the table to confirm. "It's always been a problem."

"I can see them here," Mela said suddenly. "This place is perfect. You can easily push these little tables around." The image of the warm, gleaming inside of the mill appeared in front of her inner eye. Sleet drummed on the windows, but the fire was bright inside. The room was full of Bay Harbor's rather rowdy seniors, who were pretending to play cards while really eating tortes, drinking hot chocolate with whiskey and cream, and telling each other jokes that would make the rest of the town blush.

"Sunny, it's going to be so much fun." Mela turned to her. "Imagine everyone coming here in the winter. Snow outside, a big old fire over there, casting a warm glow over the room... Bay Harbor *needs* this. We never had a place where we could gather in the winter. The restaurants are too expensive and too small for most people to go often, the Beach Bistro is closed, and you can't even meet in Beach Cove because the drive is too dangerous when the roads are icy."

"The winters are long," Peter chimed in. "Beautiful, but long. People get lonely and depressed." He cleared his throat. How lonely had he been before they found each other? Mela took his hand and squeezed it.

"Yes." Sunny sighed. "They sure are. I can see it now. I'm glad you have tables and coffee."

"Let's see the rest," Mela suggested. "Before Charlie comes back and tells us two hundred more things he wants to do."

They toured the kitchen in the back. It was modern and bright; Tom and Em had contributed their expertise, and it was set up similar to their own bakery in Beach Cove. Sunny often helped Em out when she was a hand short, and the familiarity brought back her confidence. Light sparked in her eyes as she touched the gleaming stoves and empty steel racks waiting for buns and pretzels.

"I think we should have the last round of the pie contest here," she said suddenly. "It's perfect."

"Well, did you know the former owner lived here?" Peter led them back out into the bistro area and past the fireplace. "This is how you get there." He opened a door.

Chapter 25

Sunny's eyes were unfocused, directed at everything and nothing as she sat in a ray of June sun. But Mela didn't think it was because of the pies the final round of contestants were arranging on the gleaming brass counter. Sunny was very focused when it came to *them*.

She leaned forward and whispered into Sunny's ear, "Do you want to stay after the contest and talk—just you and me?"

Sunny blinked, coming back from wherever she'd been. "If you don't mind, honey."

"Anytime." Sunny had fallen in love with the bakery, the creek, the charming apartment with its gleaming hardwood floors and antique furniture from the original mill scattered around. Mela knew in her heart Sunny wanted to live here. Maybe not for long but for as long as she could.

She kissed her aunt's cheek. She loved having Sunny at home, but even she had to admit—the mill suited her better than the small bedroom upstairs in Julie's old house. Sunny would have a beautiful ground-level apartment with an attached professional kitchen, all the space and company, and the view of the sea that was so important to her. It was a couple of miles from Seasweet Lane, most of it connected by beaches. It would be a nice morning walk to the mill for breakfast.

"I don't mind, Sunny."

Sunny looked up, her eyes searching for a moment. "Okay. Thank you."

"Anytime, auntie." Mela straightened her back and nodded at the last contestant carrying their creation into the mill's café. Mrs. Fletcher, whose son was the butcher over in Sandville. She was holding her covered pie plate like a shield in front of her as if she needed protection from the unexpected sight of the renovated mill.

"This way." Sunny waved her to the last spot on the counter, leaving Mela standing by the window.

Mela picked up her clipboard and started inspecting the pies. She wasn't a judge but was tasked with a survey. Sunny had made her a list of criteria to be checked off. After two rounds of game show-like exclusions, there were no more sunken middles, spilling goo, crumbling shells, or burned pastry crusts. These bakers were the best of the best.

Mela's nostrils flared as she walked along the line of chatting contestants, ticking off marks for golden crusts and pretty fillings. She'd had an excellent lunch of salmon, potato gratin, and tomato salad. But even though Mela wasn't hungry at all, the pies made her mouth water. Later, after Sunny announced the winners, everyone would have coffee and eat the cakes. But that was still a long way off.

From the other end of the bar, Amelie caught her eye. She grinned and waved furtively as if they were schoolgirls again, swapping secret signs in the classroom. Mela chuckled and waved back. Amelie had also been roped into judging. How many points out of ten for ease of serving the pie? Would it slide off the cake server daintily or in a gooey mess?

Mela watched as her friend's knife sunk into a pie shell. The slice came out clean, but a crumb dropped to the side. Amelie picked it up and popped it into her mouth, then made a note. Mrs. Fletcher smiled nervously.

Mela carried on. Cherry filling as vibrant as a June morning. A strawberry rhubarb pie with flaky pastry that gave off a sweet and tart scent. She swallowed, checked, and moved on. Boysenberry crumble pie with a golden, buttery crust. Check and check.

"How is it going?"

Mela looked up. "Bennett! You came!"

"And I brought everyone else." Her soon-to-be son-in-law pointed at her checklist and chuckled. "You understand that you're supposed to check only the boxes that actually apply?"

"Yes." Mela pressed the board to her chest. "It's just, all these pies are perfect. They meet all the criteria."

Bennett leaned forward. "Hot tip—Mom smuggled a pie in the lineup."

Mela exhaled. "Oh no, she didn't! Are you serious?"

"I wouldn't joke about something like this."

Mela shook her head. "She wants to win," she whispered. "She can't enter because she's a judge, but of course she wants to win! Bennett! How could you let her do that? Aren't you supposed to uphold the law?"

Bennett raised both hands. "Snitches get stitches." He squared his shoulders. "I can't wait to taste the pies. I have my eye on the chocolate-vanilla swirl cheesecake with honey-glazed almond crumble topping and cherry coulis. Don't you?"

Mela tilted her head. "Really? I had you down for the creamy blueberry-lavender custard with salted caramel and a crunchy lemon wafer crust."

The detective bowed his head like a Spanish duke. "I suppose we all err in our own little ways." He smiled thoughtfully and then left to join Sisley, who was letting Lovie touch the old millstone in the middle.

Mela's gaze brushed past the deep-dish key lime pie with a hint of raspberry and coconut flakes to land on the only cheesecake with coulis. The glazed dome, shaped to perfection, looked scrumptious—and awfully familiar. She narrowed her eyes and ticked off a box for the caramelized peach crust pecan in front of her.

Judging the pies took long enough for the sun to sink. Everyone but Sunny seemed exhausted. The new coffee maker had been tested out, and the scent of fresh, roasted beans mingled excruciatingly with that of the pies.

Sunny shuffled up to Mela, flipping through a pack of notes as thick as a thumb. "Well, well, well," she murmured, hunching over as if she needed to protect her scribbles from spies. "The savory pies are *really* pulling strong."

"Dear Aunt." By now, Mela was sitting with her daughters at one of the bistro tables. Her legs hurt from running up and down lines of pies. Maybe it was psychosomatic, though, because Sunny wasn't letting anyone eat. The crowd was becoming restless. Husbands and fathers had been forced to bring their kids outside.

"What?" Sunny looked up.

Mela tried to look stern even though her daughters were grinning. "Have you finally made up your mind?"

A critical dimple appeared in Sunny's cheek. "I can't tell if the pecan-maple-bacon pie with a hint of cayenne is a little too...hmm. And the mango curry pie—it's such a savory-sweet fusion of spices. But does it serve its function?"

Kimmie snorted a suppressed laughter.

Sunny frowned at her.

"Oh, don't look at me like that, Sunny." Kimmie spread her open hands on the table. "We want our piece of pie—everyone's waited long enough. Tell them already who won."

Sunny took a quiet breath that stuttered like a sob. "I don't know who to pick, kids," she whispered. "I've been debating it all afternoon. The three best pies are equally good. I can't pick one over the other."

"Oh no no no." Mela shook her head. "You have to! The kids have melted down, and the adults are not far behind. I saw Mrs.

Fletcher pretend she didn't see Mrs. Harris, and Mrs. Harris is starting to say Ms. Summer is jealous of her rhubarb. Please just get it over with so they all can be friends again."

"Who should I say? The cheesecake, the blueberry, or the pecan-bacon?"

"I'm fresh out of ideas, Sunny. You have to—no, wait. Not the cheesecake."

"No? Why not? I know I'll have to justify it to whoever baked it. It's unbelievable." Mela leaned forward. "Not the cheesecake. Don't place it at all."

"Mom, you can't just take a pie out of the running." Sisley stared at her.

"Trust me on this one."

"Okay. Okay." Sunny inhaled, too stressed to argue. "That does make it easier. Only two left."

Kimmie reached out and put a hand on Sunny's arm. "Give two first prizes. One for savory, one for sweet. You can't be expected to pick a side between the two."

Sunny's eyelids fluttered. "Mela?"

"Fabulous idea. Go ahead. Do it."

"Do it!" Sisley and Kimmie whispered in unison.

Sunny turned on her heel and marched to the millstone in the middle. "Listen, everyone," she called.

Immediately, the chatter died down. The bakers and their families had waited for this moment.

"All the cakes were...fantastic." Sunny sounded breathless. "I mean it. I would be proud to feature any of the recipes in this bakery."

Whoops and applause from the audience. Somebody in the back yelled, 'key lime!' but Mela couldn't see who it was.

"So when I announce the winners, I want you to know that I have not been able to sleep for days because I knew I would have to disappoint a lot of bakers who can be darn proud of themselves."

"Yeah, never mind!" another husband hollered. "I'll eat your cake anyway!"

The crowd hushed him.

Sunny cleared her throat. "After long and careful consideration, the tenth place goes to the Amarettini-cherry cream pie."

Mela propped her elbows on the table while Sunny went through her list, taking time to linger over the details of every winning pie. The girls wandered off to take turns with their kids.

A chair scraped beside her.

Mela crossed her legs. "Hello, Amelie."

"Hello again. Exciting, isn't it?" Amelie's eyes shone.

Mela lifted her chin and raised an eyebrow. "Is there something you'd like to tell me, Amelie?"

Maybe there was a glint of guilt in her friend's eye. "Like...what?"

Mela sighed. "Like any recent bad behavior on your part? *Terrible* behavior, in fact? To do with cherry coulis?"

Amelie's lips pressed together. "How did you know?" she hissed. "I was so careful smuggling it in."

"You're helping Sunny judge! What do you think happens if anyone else finds out? Sunny poured her heart into this—and she's going to run the bakery! People would be so mad if they found out."

Amelie leaned back. "I wasn't going to do anything." She looked at her hands. "I didn't think it would get out. I just wanted to participate."

Mela shook her head. "I told Sunny not to pick the cheesecake."

"Really?"

"Yes."

Amelie inhaled a big breath, held it, and then blew it out. "Some friend you are, Pamela."

"You're welcome. What if Sunny had announced it was yours?" She leaned closer. "What were you planning on doing if you won and Sunny's calling for the baker? Stand up? Run away?"

"I put in a fake name."

"Oh Amelie. For real? You think the ladies would not put two and two together?"

Amelie cleared her throat. A faint flush warmed her cheeks. "Anyway. You blew my cover."

Mela shook her head. "Maybe you can't help it. Maybe it's in your genes."

"I suppose it is." For a while, they sat silently, listening to Sunny and joining into the applause. "Um. Thank you, Mela."

Mela shook her head, still hardly able to believe Amelie would be so invested in baking she would put Sunny in a tough spot. But then she sighed. "I've got your back, girlfriend."

There was another pause. Then, "Top contender, huh?" Amelie said.

"Yep. Top contender."

Amelie's elbow gently connected with Mela's ribs. "Hey.

"What?"

"I got caught up in the game. It was stupid of me. Thanks for keeping me on the straight and narrow. I mean it."

Mela smiled back. "Anytime."

"And now," Sunny's voice rose over the applauding, whistling crowd, "let the eating begin!"

Chapter 26

"Where do you want this box?"

"That goes into the bedroom if you don't mind, Travis." Kitty straightened and wiped a curl out of her face. She was ready for a cold drink, but there were still boxes coming in. Luckily, most of them had still been unopened, and they only had to bring them from the rented roof apartment to her beach house.

Her beach house...

Travis changed his grip on the heavy book box. "Not a problem, ma'am."

"Thank you. I think we're almost done."

"Auntie Kitty!" Pippa came running to her, throwing her arms around her knees. "Can I live here too?"

Kitty smiled. "You already get to live with Kimmie and your dad. But I'm sure you can sleep over sometimes."

"Can Brooke have a sleepover too?"

"Brooke is too young to have sleepovers. But when she gets older, we can ask her grandma Sam if it's okay."

"Can we cook something fancy?"

Kitty laughed. "I think sleeping over at Auntie Amelie's is better for that one. I'm not much of a cook. But we could have a beach fire and roast s'mores. That is, only if you like chocolate and marshmallows and crackers. If you don't, we'll roast...carrots!"

"Carrots?" Pippa giggled. "Can you read me a book?"

"Right now?"

Mela and Kimmie had caught the last words. "How about we let Auntie Kitty move in first?" Mela said mildly.

Kimmie set a tote bag of spices on the counter. She squatted to be on the level of her daughter and took her hands. "Miss Alice told me she's found a new book for you. How about the two of us go and check out the beach until she gets here?"

"Okay." Pippa suddenly yanked her hands out of Kimmie's and slung them around her neck. "Carry me!"

"Kimmie can't carry you, big girl." Travis, relieved of his box, scooped his daughter into his arms and stood. "I'm coming too."

"Yaya! Right now! Right now!"

"Kimmie?"

Kimmie rose. "I'm just going to use the bathroom and catch up."

Travis turned to Kitty. "Bennett, Peter, and Charlie are bringing what's left. The van was almost empty."

Kitty nodded. "Thank you, Travis. I owe you a big old Piña Colada on that front porch."

"Dibs on the hammock." Travis leaned over and kissed Kitty's cheek. "See ya."

"Bye."

They all waved back at Pippa as she was being carried outside, and Kimmie hurried to the bathroom.

Kitty leaned on the counter. "Did you hear that?" she whispered.

"Hear what? Which part?" Mela whispered back.

"The part where she can't lift anything right now."

"Hmm. Didn't she carry boxes?"

"Only totes. Not that I mind, that's not what I'm saying. But then Travis said she couldn't carry Pippa." Kitty lowered her chin significantly.

Mela looked at the tote of loose spices as if it had any answers. "She's strong enough to carry Pippa, isn't she? She's done it lots of times."

"I know."

"Maybe she's tired. Pippa still doesn't sleep well. She still misses her mother."

"Of course she does." Kitty patted her sister's hand on the island. "But I don't think that's why Kimmie has to pee every two seconds. I don't think that's why she can't lift her baby." She leaned closer at the same time as Mela. Their faces were only inches apart. "*Baby*. Get it?"

"Whaaaa—" Mela's eyes opened slowly, all the way, and then some more. "No."

The faint sound of water flushing was audible.

Kitty leaned back and pulled the tote bag closer. "I can feel it in my bones." She pulled out a jar of cinnamon and held it up as if it were proof.

"What's with the cinnamon?" Kimmie entered the kitchen. She looked tired, and there were pale blue shadows under her eyes.

Mela tapped her fingers on the counter. "Hmm. Kimmie?"

"Yes?"

"Is there...something?"

A short pause. "Like?"

Kitty threw caution to the wind. "Like something you want to share with us, your concerned female relatives, who have your best interest at heart?

"You don't have to, but you can if you like," Mela added.

Kimmie closed her eyes. A smile spread slowly over her face. She opened her eyes again. "I'm almost at the end of the first trimester."

"I knew it!" Kitty laughed. "Mela!"

Mela stirred back to life. "Really? Oh honey." She took Kimmie's face in her hands and kissed her daughter's forehead. "Wow. Are you happy? I'm so happy. Are you happy?"

"I'm very happy." Kimmie laughed. "What gave me away?"

"Little things here and there. Being nauseated. Having to pee all the time. Not lifting things." Kitty hugged her niece. "Let's sit down before your mom collapses."

"Good idea," Mela said weakly. "I can't believe it's real. Tell me everything." She sat at the kitchen island, and Kimmie and Kitty followed her example.

"Well, now the cat's out of the bag." Kimmie laughed. "Where to start? Not at the very beginning!"

"What?" Mela sounded breathless. She looked at Kitty and back at her daughter, then smacked her lips as if her mouth was dry.

"Orange juice," Kitty decided and opened her new fridge. "And prosecco for everyone who's made it to menopause. I inherited some nice champagne flutes from the previous owner." She put the juice and prosecco on the counter and opened the cabinets. "I don't know my way around yet. Ah, there they are."

"I want a strong one." Mela sounded better. Kitty smiled at her sister and obliged.

"You have no idea how much I wanted to tell you, Mom." Kimmie took her orange juice. "I almost did a million times."

"Here's to mother and baby." Kitty lifted her glass. She had barely moved in, and they were already making unforgettable memories.

"Cheers!" Her sister and niece lifted their glasses too, and they drank. Mela emptied her glass, and Kitty refilled it.

"Easy, Mom. I've got something for you." Kimmie lifted off the chair to reach for something in the back pocket of her jeans. "Look at this."

She laid an unmistakable black-and-white photo on the counter. Mela picked it up. "You already had an ultrasound!"

"I went last week," Kimmie announced. "Travis and I saw the heartbeat. The ultrasound technician said everything looked good." She smiled at the memory.

Mela turned the photo so Kitty could see. "Oh! There it is!"

"Just a little bean with a heart." Out of nowhere, tears welled up in Kitty's eyes. "I'm so happy for you." Kitty wasn't sure whether she was talking to Mela or Kimmie or the bean—or maybe herself. "He's going to have so many kids to play with—and so much family ready to love him."

"He?" Kimmie laughed. "It's rather too early to say."

Mela drained her glass again but put her hand over it so Kitty couldn't refill. Mela's next words came cautiously. "Is Travis happy?"

Kimmie looked up, surprise in her eyes. "Of course he's happy." She bit her lip. "Mom—he's happy. He wants a family as much as I do. With me."

Mela's chest rose and sank, and Kitty knew her sister struggled. "Sorry," she said then, sounding sincere. "Once a mama bear, always a mama bear. I know he's happy. Of course I do. It was just a reflex."

Kitty had heard about Travis's disappearing act. Mela had told her that much as she wanted to, she didn't quite trust her ex-son-in-law to stick around.

"I understand." Kimmie rubbed her cheek. "It's never going to be the way it used to between Travis and me."

Mela glanced at Kitty, and Kitty nodded. Whatever it was Kimmie needed, they had her back. "If anything happens between the two of you... We're here for you, honey. You don't have to tough it out with him if it's not everything you wanted."

Kimmie looked at her mom, then Kitty, then back at her mom. "I meant that Travis and I are in a different place now. It's better. It's *so* much better."

Mela nodded. "It's only... Well, it's just..." She raised an eyebrow at her daughter. "Has he asked you to marry him?"

"No, he hasn't." Kimmie looked surprised. "But I don't care. I can ask him myself if I want to."

"I think maybe I've waited long enough for you to do it."

Their heads swiveled to the open door. Travis stood there, his daughter in his arms. How much had he overheard?

"Well, how about it?" He came inside and put down Pippa, who went to stand by Mela's knee and watched with wide eyes.

Travis had eyes only for Kimmie. "I was going to wait for a romantic moment. Something special, something better than the first time I asked." He reached out.

Kimmie got off her chair and gave him her hand. "But?" Kimmie smiled.

"But the moment was never good enough. Like you said, we're different now. What we have is different. It is no longer going to be candlelight dinners sprinkled in between long absences. We no longer risk our lives for some words on a front page." Travis smiled back. "Now it's watching cartoons in the afternoon and taking turns holding our daughter when she has nightmares. It's long beach walks with the family. It's...it's love everywhere. And you..." Travis lowered himself to one knee and pulled a velvet box from the pocket of his windbreaker.

"Oh." Kimmie's lips trembled.

"You are at the center of it. You are the heart of my life. I love you, Kimmie." Travis opened the box, and a diamond glinted. "Will you marry me—again?"

A sob escaped Kitty's niece. "Stupid hormones," she said and wiped her eyes with the back of her hand. "Yes. Yes, of course I'll marry you again."

Travis exhaled, and his head sunk to his chest as if the words made him dizzy. Then he stood and pulled the diamond from its cushion.

Kimmie held out her hand, and he slipped the ring on it. She gave him a watery smile. "I love you too, Trav."

He pulled her to him and kissed her, long and lingering.

Kitty grinned, slipped off her chair, and grabbed the bottle of prosecco and her glass. "Congratulations! I'm so happy for you both." She nodded for Mela to come.

"Congratulations, you two. I can't believe... I'm so, so happy." Mela's voice wavered as if she was going to cry too, but then she took Pippa's hand and followed Kitty onto the porch.

Kitty slid the door shut behind them. "Let's just give them a moment." She giggled at the look on her sister's face. "You need a moment too. Did you bring your glass?"

"Yes." Mela held it out. "Pippa, there are juice boxes on the backseat of my car. The doors are open. Can you go get one?"

"Yes! Are they going to get married?"

"Do you want them to?"

"Brooke and I wrote wishes on paper and buried them on the beach. I wrote, "I want Daddy and Kimmie to marry."

"Brooke can *write*?" Mela asked weakly.

"Yeah, but she wrote that she wants to be a fish. I'll get juice." Pippa ran off.

Kitty refilled their own glasses. "Let's look at the ocean for a bit. Let it sink in. I want to savor the moment."

"Yes."

Kimmy and Travis came out laughing and holding hands. They all hugged and kissed, and then the young couple joined their daughter on the beach. Pippa handed Travis her juice and started searching the washed-up seaweed for shells, sand dollars, and sea urchins. Travis and Kimmie sat side by side in the sand. He put his arm around her, and she leaned her head on his shoulder.

Kitty smiled. "Our view just got that much better, didn't it? Here. Let's sit on the porch stairs." She lowered herself onto the top stair and patted the spot beside her. Mela joined her. "Cheers." Kitty held out her glass.

Her sister clinked. "Cheers. Here's to all of it. Baby, marriage, happy kids, and new houses."

Kitty lay on the porch, squinting into the blue sky. "I don't know what happened. I thought I was okay. That I liked my life. But then I came to Bay Harbor."

"I've had too much to drink." Mela lay back as well, turning her head. Kitty felt her sister's eyes on her. "But same. Weird."

"It's weird how I didn't know better. And it is weird how fast things change. Like the clouds up there." Kitty pointed her flute at the white wisps. "Like commas in the sky."

Mela giggled. "Commas in the sky. You're dry. Drunk, I mean."

Kitty had to giggle too. "*You* are."

"Are you two all right?"

"Oh! Oof." Kitty snapped into a sitting position again.

Bennett and Sisley stood on the sand, eyeing them curiously. Baby Lovie, sitting on her dad's arm, put a finger in her mouth.

"I'm dizzy," Mela said. "Join us."

Sisley sat on the lowest stair, and Bennett set Lovie on the sand. The toddler lifted her feet to inspect the sand on the soles of her feet. "Shells," she said and took off in Pippa's direction to help with the beach combing.

"She just said shells." Bennett stared at Sisley. "She just said shells!"

Sisley stared back. "She did!"

Bennett ran a hand through his hair. "She's so smart. She's going to be such a good detective."

Sisley laughed, and then she asked why Mela and Kitty were lying drunk and giggling on the porch, and when they finally all went back into the kitchen because it was getting hot, Travis and Kimmie were still sitting in the sand, holding each other.

"You know what?" Sisley opened the fridge and pulled out a quiche for lunch. "I think this time, it'll last."

"I think so too," Kitty said.

"And I agree," Mela said and went to get glasses for Bennett and Sisley as well.

Chapter 27

The heavy wooden door of the small white church opened. Sunlight streamed in like a bright carpet, and Mela, her heart beating in her throat, turned to look.

There was a collective holding-of-breath, a wait that connected them all, an expectation they all shared. Everyone was ready to see the bride.

Especially Bennett.

His best man handed him a tissue. Bennett uncrossed his hands behind his back and took it, dabbing his jaw just below his ear as if he'd forgotten how to use a tissue. His eyes never left the door. Smiling, his best man—another detective from the homicide squad—tugged the tissue out of Bennett's hand and put it in his pocket.

Mela's fingers closed around her own tissue. Her eyes met Robert's, and he put a hand on hers. "I love you," he mouthed.

She nodded. She loved him too. Not like she loved Peter, deep and passionately and forever, but the way she'd loved her ex-husband all along. They had this beautiful daughter together, and he'd witnessed Sisley growing up. Mela was glad he was present.

With them, in the very front, sat Sunny and Kitty, Travis, Peter, and Robert's new wife, Leonora. They were all on good terms with each other, all grateful that the past had taken the turns and twists it needed to take.

On the other side of the aisle sat the groom's party; Amelie, her mother Meredith, and Charlie. Meredith had reserved a spot for

Pippa because that's where the little girl had announced she was going to sit, and she was also going to hold Lovie because Lovie would want to sit where Pippa was.

Friends and neighbors filled the rest of the church. Maisie, Sam, Ellie, and Cate had all brought their partners and children and grandchildren. Martin's good friends, the fishermen of Beach Cove, stood hats in hand in the back to see his great-granddaughter walk down the aisle because he couldn't.

Mela spotted her kids' real estate agents, Ian and Kelly, who were holding hands, and Alice Harper, who had become Pippa's beloved babysitter. The entire senior canasta club had squeezed into two benches to not hog space, sitting arms hooked in with each other so they would fit. Bennett's cop friends from Cape Bass did the same minus the arms, and the Botrels had brought grandma and kids.

There were many more. All of them were rooting for Sisley's and Bennett's happiness, filling the air with their energy so it practically vibrated with their good wishes and love.

"When is she coming?" Kimmie whispered audibly. "What is she waiting for?"

Kitty exhaled and glanced at the bridegroom. "Has he blinked yet?" she whispered back. "His eyes are going to dry out."

"There they are!" Robert put his hands together as if he wanted to applaud.

A collective *awww* went through the crowd. Pippa and Brooke appeared in the light like tiny walking cream puffs, pulling Lovie, who sat in a white beach buggy filled with the flowers. All three were adorable in matching pink tulle and flowered headbands that Lovie was trying to pull off. Brooke pushed it back, and Lovie swatted at her hand.

"Come on," Sunny murmured. It'd been her job to teach the girls what to do. "Start walking! You can do it, darlings!"

"Naah!" Lovie's sturdy legs in their white tights kicked, and she reached out. "Dada!"

Bennett's intake of air made everyone turn to him. He took a shuddering breath for all to see. "Smart girl," he mouthed.

"You're supposed to throw flowers!" Pippa hissed in a whisper that echoed around the church.

Mela smiled, and people giggled behind their hands, delighted at the cute spectacle. Every last soul present witnessed it.

Pippa tossed a handful of petals on the ground.

Sunny half-rose and waved them to come forward. "Walk, honey!" she whisper-called. "Come on!" She made a gesture to show Brooke and Pippa should sprinkle the flowers. Brooke looked into her basket as if noticing for the first time it was filled and set it down. Lovie pouted, her little hands still grasping for her dad.

Bennett turned to his best friend, and the man set off at a jog down the aisle, lifted Lovie, and brought her back to the front of the church. Bennett whispered to Lovie and put her on the stairs by his feet, where she sat like a little stone statue wearing bloomers.

"You have to walk!" Sunny called to the girls, not trying to be quiet anymore. "Come on!"

People started laughing, and then someone else was laughing too, her voice clear and happy. Tears shot into Mela's eyes, and she pressed the tissue to her lips.

Sisley appeared in the doorway, her graceful silhouette outlined against the bright light.

Another collective gasp went through the church as they spotted the radiant bride.

"She's beautiful," Robert said hoarsely. "When did she become so beautiful?"

"Come on, girls," Sisley said and held out a hand to each little flower sprinkler. "We'll go together."

The girls obediently took her hands, and the three walked slowly down the aisle as the organ broke into a jubilant rendition of *here comes the bride*.

Tears were dripping on Mela's cheeks. There was nothing she could do to stop it. She waved when her daughter passed, and for the first time, Sisley's face fell. Her lips trembled, and in an instant, she looked like the little girl that had skinned her knee and wanted her mom. Mela blew her a kiss as images from Sisley's childhood flooded back.

Sisley nodded, and the smile returned. She blew a quick kiss back and walked the rest of the way to the altar, where she gently pried Brooke and Pippa off her dress and pointed them toward Amelie. Lovie unfroze and went to sit with her friends.

Sisley went to the middle of the aisle, smoothed her skirt and her veil, and lifted her bouquet of hydrangeas. Then she winked cheekily at Bennett. Mela hoped his best man was strong enough to hold him up should he pass out from the wink. It looked like he might.

Another sigh went through the gatherers, this one coming from deep inside their hearts. Everyone saw the love Bennett felt because it was plainly written on his face. Everyone remembered the feeling—if not from experience, then from dipping into the endless well of shared humanity. Tears started to flow freely, and more than one tissue flashed white as Sisley handed her bouquet to Kimmie and stood to face Bennett.

The pastor started to speak, and everyone fell silent as the familiar words bound Sisley and Bennett together forever.

For a moment, Mela closed her eyes. The flowers in the centerpieces smelled like the garden of her mother's house, their vibrant perfume filling the air and making her heart ache for Julie.

A tear ran down her cheek, and Kitty, sitting beside her, took her hand. Mela wrapped her fingers around her sister's, for support, for comfort, for connection. When she opened her eyes again, Sisley, radiant with happiness, leaned in to kiss the love of her life.

"Everything will be all right." Kitty took Mela's hand. "Everything will be good."

Thank you for reading Seaside Ties! If you want to read more, Beach Cove Home is where the story of Maisie, Ellie, Sam and Cate starts – long before they met the ladies of Bay Harbor. After a decade away, Maisie returns to her old home in the small seaside town. She's on a desperate mission, but the friends she neglected so long are still there for her.

Continue for a sample of Beach Cove Home

Beach Cove Home

Chapter One

The sea sent her great rushing waters into the bay; the bay settled the surge and channeled it into the cove. The cove, calm and sapphirine, comforted what remained of the Atlantic's temper so that the waves lapped at the sandy beaches like kittens drinking milk.

Maisie rounded the last curve in the road as the sun settled into the highest branches of the pine trees. She slowed the white Acura to the speed of windswept houses, crying gulls, and rambling gardens.

For ten long years, she'd avoided the oyster-shaped cove that carved itself—warmer than it had any right to be—into Maine's rugged shoreline. She'd avoided the small town of Beach Cove that sat like a pearl at the tip of the cove, avoided picturing the sandy beaches that gave the cove its name, the fishing boats and lobster vessels bobbing in the harbor, the quaint shops sprinkled throughout the few streets like nuggets of sea glass.

She had more important things to do than drown in memories, so she'd avoided all of it.

Until she couldn't. Until the call of duty came, and she had to return.

Only for a brief time, though. Two days, maybe three. No more. She'd do what she had to do, give the interview, point out the places, answer the same old questions, and if she was lucky, some new ones.

She wasn't there to visit. She would not get in touch with anyone or check to see what remained of the town she'd moved to as a young bride, eager to start a family and be happy. She was simply going to slip in and out.

Her place was in New York City. Besides offering the infrastructure she needed, the Big Apple was a conglomerate of glittering distractions. Sleepy little Beach Cove, with its lazy morning mists and endless afternoons, was not.

But Maisie needed the noise of the City to drown out her thoughts. There were ringing phones to answer, deadlines to meet, desperate people to talk to, and stacks of documents covering her desk. So much work; important work. It forced her mind into a narrow one-way street. It kept her from straying into the dark.

Slowing to a crawl, Maisie entered the historic village. It was the heart of Beach Cove, as important to the town as a diamond to an engagement ring. Maisie stole glances left and right as she passed by the shop windows she used to browse and the doors she used to walk through.

Everything seemed the same...only a little *off*. Like an acquaintance Maisie couldn't place. Familiar, but out of context. In her head, she'd changed the place into something that didn't altogether match reality. Now, the village pulled on her mind, pushing it back into a shape it hadn't taken in a long time.

When she reached the far side of the village, Maisie released a pent-up breath and turned into the narrow road that led toward the house. There were the same gray Cape-Cod style houses still... The front yard hydrangeas were coming into their May greenery, the young leaves waving as Maisie passed.

It wasn't long until houses became sparse and finally trickled away. Sand started to replace soil. Gardens gave way to a different sort of beauty as native plants claimed their place. Tufts of yellow beach heather widened into swaths, their tiny flowers coaxed into bloom by the mild spring. Here and there, tussocks of little bluestem and pinweed interrupted the blooming sprawl of heather. Adding its tribute to the cove's beauty, the sinking sun streaked the evening sky in matching shades of lavender and lilac.

By the time Maisie pulled into the gravel driveway, climbed out of the car, and took her first deep breath of the salty air, everything had snapped back into place. She knew Beach Cove again. She knew it intimately, like an old friend she'd missed all along.

Maisie closed her eyes to shut out the feeling, but losing the images only awakened her other senses. The sea breeze lifted the hair off her shoulders and brushed her hands with the tenderness of a lover. The dry kelp flavoring the air, the melodies of breaking waves and rustling seagrass, the red-winged blackbird trilling its evening song...

Maisie blinked. That had done no good at all. Wiping a hair out of her face, she eyed the tall brick house at the end of the driveway, gathering courage. It seemed to her that the light of a happier past must shine behind the closed shutters.

But of course, it was all dark inside. Beach House had stood empty for ten years.

Maisie pulled her suitcase from the trunk and walked to the house. The key with the silver whale pendant was tarnished from neglect, but it unlocked the front door without complaint.

Maisie touched a fingertip to the wood. She'd painted it herself. Silk Sophistication in Carmine Excitement. The girls had giggled over the outlandish name, but it'd been the shade both she and Robert had liked best. Red because soon after they'd bought the house, Maisie had found in a magazine that a red door was an olden-day signal for weary travelers to rest the horse and stay the night.

She'd stay only a couple of nights. No longer.

Maisie pushed the door open and stepped inside. A sigh of dry rosewood and dusty marble brushed past, escaping into the night.

Maisie waited until it was gone before she closed the door behind her. She set down her suitcase and flicked on the light.

Everything was the same. There was the dent in the floorboard where Alex had dropped his skates. There was the chandelier, dripping with crystals and too high to be dusted properly. The mahogany board and mirror on the wall, the green cast-iron coat tree nobody ever used. Maisie turned to the arched floor-to-ceiling windows that framed the central staircase on the far side. Beyond the windows, the overgrown lawn swept toward the beach and finally the sea.

The sea.

Maisie walked across for a better view.

The sea, always hungry, was busy swallowing the sun, and the fading light tinted the sand an unlikely anthracite. Beach grass smudged into sand, sand into sea. The only spots of color came from the white-crested waves far out, where the bay washed through craggy cliffs into the cove.

May was early yet for Maine. But in the cove, spring, this reluctant transition from barren winter to the tourist-luring glory of summer, had long started to whisper across the water and kiss the coast.

Maisie loved spring. She'd loved all the seasons here.

The first jellyfish of spring, the summer heat that brought guests and open-air concerts, the heart-achingly gorgeous fall when the tourists finally left and the small town settled back on its heels to take a breath. Then winter, beautiful and lonely and never-ending, bringing out the grit in those that stayed after the charm of wood fires and hot tea had worn thin.

Maisie had loved it all.

Until.

Slackening one finger at a time, Maisie pulled off her leather gloves. They helped with the pain in the joints of her hands after typing too many emails too many days in a row, and she'd needed them for the long drive. But they wouldn't be good here where the air vibrated with salt and sand and the whispering mist snuck between the fibers of wool and leather.

She probably still had some nylon gloves in the basement closet, though it was unlikely she'd need them. Last evening's forecast had predicted a freak heatwave for Maine, so Maisie hadn't packed much. Certainly nothing warm enough for a breezy beach walk, should the forecast turn out to be wrong.

Maisie shook her head once at the window, telling the view to stop tempting her. She wasn't planning on beach walks, even though she used to love them. Especially in the early morning, before the family woke. Letting the clear water tickle her toes and her heels sink into the sand. Admiring what treasure the sea had brought her.

But the sea also took what it wanted.

Maisie cut that train of thought and returned to her suitcase. Her job was to keep her head and to stay focused. Families relied on her clear thinking when their world dove into a whirlpool of panic. Most of all, Alex needed her. Not brooding or taking anguished beach walks, but acting calm, efficient, and—

Her cell phone rang, the shrill sound startling Maisie into a hasty pat-down of her coat pockets. "Hello?"

"Mrs. Jameson?" The voice was male.

"Yes, speaking."

"It's Jim Andersen. From the Lost Souls podcast?"

Jim always sounded apologetic, as if he was afraid Maisie thought he was exploiting her heartbreak for his own purpose.

In a way, he was.

But the deal ran two ways.

Maisie clutched the phone tighter. The connection was breaking up. Beach Cove liked to swallow radio waves. "Jim. How are you?"

"Yeah, good." Jim cleared his throat in an embarrassed staccato. Maybe he thought he had no business being good when talking to her. "Is it too late to talk?"

"It's barely evening. Go ahead." Maisie shimmied out of her navy trench coat and tossed it onto the walnut chair Robert had inherited from an aunt in France. While Jim spun polite introductory wool, Maisie also kicked off her sneakers and made her way into the kitchen.

Here, too, nothing seemed to have changed. Other than being a little dustier and a lot tidier than when Maisie had kept house. She opened a cabinet.

Robert had left Maisie plenty of fancy wine, even though he hadn't managed to leave her a note. She searched until she found a cabernet; the label told her nothing beyond that. Her husband had been the connoisseur, not she. She'd simply enjoyed what he'd poured.

She'd never paid enough attention to anything. Not even the wine labels.

"Mm-hmm." Maisie rummaged on until she found a corkscrew and a glass that she dusted with the sleeve of her button-down shirt.

"Anyway." Jim had worked his way to the actual purpose of his call. "I could have the team in Beach Cove, like, tomorrow?"

"Fine." Holding the phone between cheek and shoulder, Maisie jerked the cork out of the bottle neck. "How many are you, exactly?"

"Like, five." Jim coughed. "Is there a motel or something?"

Maisie poured herself a glass. He wanted to come tomorrow and hadn't yet looked up places to stay? Hopefully, he'd turn out to be a better sleuth than that promised... His email had said he was an investigative reporter, but there'd been no official header or footer that showed he came from a reputable news outlet.

Not that it mattered. She'd take whoever she could get. Whoever wanted to help. Jim was fine. He had a platform.

"We don't have hotels or even motels near Beach Cove. There used to be a few inns a couple of towns over, but as far as I know, they're closed this time of year. So are the B&Bs." Maisie lifted the glass to her lips and swallowed.

Sour!

She spat the wine into the sink, frowning at the burgundy rivulets of vinegar. "You can stay with me if you bring sleeping bags. The house is big enough to be an inn, but I don't know what the linen situation is. If there are any, they're dusty. Or moldy."

"Well no, we don't want to bother you. I didn't mean to fish for an invitation and—"

"Nonsense." Maisie stepped on the trash can pedal and tossed her glass in. It hit the metal, the long stem snapping with a satisfying crunch. She sighed. Nothing about being in Beach House was going to be easy, least of all controlling her emotions. "Don't be silly; there's nowhere else to stay. You can help out and make breakfast."

Jim hemmed, but when she didn't respond, he eventually said, "Okay. Thank you, Mrs. Jameson, that sounds great. We'll bring eggs and bacon."

"I'm too old for bacon."

"Oh, sure. Do you like bagels and cream cheese?"

"Coffee would be good." Eating had become strictly functional. At fifty-two, Maisie finally was that skinny stick who could wear anything off the rack. But it wasn't worth it by a long shot. If she could, she'd take back her pleasure in food. And her curves.

"Coffee. Got it." Jim sounded conciliatory. "We'll see you tomorrow morning then?"

"Don't be very late, if you can. I don't want to be here, least of all on my own. Just me and this place—that doesn't work so well."

"I understand. I'll make sure we'll get there early, Mrs. Jameson. Thanks for the invitation. Take care."

"You, too." Maisie ended the call.

A whole night ahead of her, quiet, and dark, and *quiet*. No flashing lights, no drunken yelling in the street, no midnight-laughter or honking to break the silence.

Maisie picked her phone back up. She had audiobooks to keep her company and she used them all the time, even if she wasn't in the mood for a book. She tapped, and an authoritative narrator picked up mid-sentence, reading from a daily news digest.

Tucking her phone into the pocket of her jeans, Maisie got her suitcase and carried it upstairs. Time to catch up on email.

The mahogany steps creaked in all the same places.

She'd meant to stay in one of the guestrooms. But if Jim was going to bring four or five people with who-knew-what sleeping arrangements, they'd need the guestrooms to spread out.

So it was the master bedroom for her after all.

Maisie padded down the high hall—Beach House had been built back in the day when heating bills must've been considered fun and dusting kept you elastic—and stepped into the old bedroom.

Her and Robert's old bedroom.

She opened the door with a quick push and looked inside. The curtains on the window moved as if someone had brushed against them, dust motes rising from the hand-laced batiste into the dim light.

It was only the door that had moved the air.

Maisie set her suitcase down.

There was the carved rosewood bed, the slim vase of blue Spode on her nightstand. Robert had put a new flower in it every night.

From the day of her wedding to the day their son disappeared.

She'd been happy here.

They all had been so happy here.

Back in the kitchen, Maisie switched on the recessed light over the sink, then off again. Darker was better. Night had fallen entirely, and bright light just made the empty kitchen feel cavernous.

The old gas range—top of the line thirty years ago but long since outdated by electronic devices so sharp they did all but the eating—hissed to life. Maisie let the flame burn for a moment, though she didn't have anything to cook. There was propane in the tank, then.

Thanks to Liz, Maisie had gas, electricity, and water. Maisie had hired the young woman to check on the house now and then. Liz kept an eye on the carpenter ants in the woodwork, made sure the roof didn't leak, and shut off the water when the temperatures dropped.

Maisie tried to peer through the French doors into the sunroom, but it was too dark to see anything other than her reflection. The garden was out there. Used to be, anyway. Liz watched the house, but she had kids and a proper job as an accountant. She wouldn't have been able to take on the garden, even if Maisie had thought to ask.

But it hadn't even occurred to her. The garden wasn't a turn-on-the-sprinkler job. Every plant had an opinion about soil, pruning, watering, timing. Maintaining it took hours, and well-off as Robert had left Maisie, she didn't splurge on hiring a gardener. She only had to keep Beach House—old, rambling, and impossibly high-taxed as it was—until Alex found his way back there.

Tomorrow morning, she'd make herself a cup of coffee. She'd hold on to it as she surveyed the damage. Maybe not all was lost. Maybe at least the boxwood had survived the decade of neglect...and possibly the roses?

Maisie closed her eyes and breathed the pictures of the past away like a painful contraction.

Don't go there.

She had rules. Simple, but dearly paid for with experience.

Don't remember. Don't imagine. Don't speculate.

Those were the rules on top of the list; the most important ones. They were the hardest ones, too.

Maisie shook her hair out of her face. A single shoulder-length strand sailed through the air and landed on her sleeve. She picked it up and rolled it between her fingertips. When she'd left Beach Cove, she'd been blonde, courtesy of the sun and the salty air. Beach-bleach blond, Robert had called the color.

That was over. Now she was gray.

Maisie knew Robert wouldn't have liked it. Not dying her hair felt like a benign act of revenge, even though it had nothing to do with him and everything with the fact that she couldn't be bothered.

Maisie tapped the trash can open and let the hair flutter inside. It settled on the shards.

She shouldn't have broken the glass—antique crystal, inherited by Robert from a rich European uncle or cousin. Maisie couldn't remember because she'd never met them; she'd never met anyone other than Robert's parents and sister. Once for the wedding, once for the funeral. The Jamesons weren't warm people by a long shot. Robert had grown up in boarding schools, the relationship with his parents summed up in a yearly settling of tuition and a monthly letter to practice penmanship and composition or some such.

Then again, Robert was gone and had left Maisie everything. It didn't matter if she broke all the glasses. The Jamesons sure didn't care.

She opened the cupboard and the fridge, taking stock. Liz had come through. Sort of. Tonight's dinner could be either a bowl of frosted flakes or ramen noodles.

Maisie fished out the hot pink pack of wheat noodles and weighed it in her hand. She didn't mind ramen, but she wanted enough calories to get through the night. If hunger woke her, she'd lie awake for hours. She'd have to fight hard to stick to her rules.

Suddenly starving, she squinted at the label, then put the pack back. It wasn't enough. She picked up her phone, found a restaurant she didn't recognize that delivered, and called.

"Beach Cove Corner Café, Tom here. How can I help you?"

The voice was familiar; the name matched. Ellie's son. Maisie closed her eyes. She'd called Tommy, of all people.

"Hello?"

"I'd like to order a cheese pizza for delivery, please. Large." It might as well last her a few meals. "A bottle of wine, too. Red, if you have any. I'm on Seashore Lane."

There was a small pause, filled with background clanging and distant voices. "Mrs. Jameson? Is that you, Mrs. Jameson?"

Maisie opened her eyes again. "Hello, Tommy. You work at a restaurant now?"

"Better, Mrs. Jameson. I own the restaurant. Are you back?"

"Only for a couple of days."

"In your house?" He sounded as if Alex had pulled out a coveted new video game, or Robert offered to take the boys sailing.

"I'm in my house," Maisie confirmed. "How are you, Tom? I had no idea—" He owned a café? But of course, he did. He'd grown up.

Tom skipped the small talk. "My mom will want to see you," he said, his voice warm with conviction. "Did you tell her you're back?"

"Uh." Maisie put a hand to her forehead. When she spoke, the words came out too hasty. "No, it's only a spur-of-the-moment thing, and I'm not staying. Tommy, can I order a pizza, please? I'm starving."

"Oh. You certainly can, Mrs. Jameson. What can I get you?"

Maisie repeated her order and ended the call.

All of twenty minutes in Beach Cove, and the town had found her out.

Chapter Two

"Mom, you'll never guess who just called."

Ellie, phone pressed between cheek and shoulder, lowered the lemon sole onto a layer of ice. It was a beautiful fish, a perfect, shimmering oval molded by the sea.

Even though Ellie had run the Beach Cove Fish for most of her adult life, it still surprised her when she had fish left over at the end of the day. Who wouldn't snap up this beauty while they could? It made no sense.

"Sweetheart, how would I know who called you. Dad?" It'd be newsworthy indeed if Dale had called. His own son, too.

Ellie picked up the second sole, as glossy and perfect as the first, and added it to the cooler bag. Hopefully, the lemons she'd bought last week were still good. Lemon juice, maybe a little peel, in a light cream sauce would be perfection. Had to be real lemon though, the stuff in that little yellow squirt thing was too acidic. Sole had such a delicate flavor.

"You know your friend from the brick house by the sea?" Tom's voice ebbed in and out, which meant he was kneading dough, phone pressed between cheek and shoulder. Like mother, like son.

Ellie looked up. The brick house. "Maisie?"

"Yep."

"Maisie called? You?" Ellie cleared her throat. "She called you? Are you serious?"

"Yes. I knew right away it was her. She's got that soft voice like she's—"

"Oh my." Ellie turned on the faucet to wash her hands. "Maisie, huh? What could she possibly want from you?"

Her son scoffed. "Thanks, Mom."

Ellie laughed. "I didn't mean it like that. I love you. Everybody loves you."

"Sure they do."

"Come on, spill. Don't leave me hanging." Ellie shut off the water and dried her hands. Tom was the same age as Alex, Maisie's son. The two of them had grown up together, been best friends. Was that why Maisie was calling Tom? Her thoughts began to whirr like an outboard motor spinning dry air.

"She didn't actually call me. She called the Café, and she didn't even say her name. But of course I know her voice and the address, so I asked if it was her."

"Are you kidding me," Ellie said again. So Maisie hadn't called Tom specifically, so that was...good? "What did she say?"

"She wanted a pizza."

"No!" Ellie slapped the counter. It stung, and she shook out her fingers. Then she ripped off a paper towel and rubbed the handprint away. "Tom, are you saying she ordered one? For here? She's in Beach Cove?"

"Yep," Tom said easily. "Anyway, gotta go."

Ellie ignored this. The kid was twenty-six, and he still couldn't resist teasing her. "She said she's at the house?"

"Yes, she's at her house. At least she ordered a pizza to be delivered to her house. In Beach Cove. The one with the garden."

"Yes, I know which house. Listen, I guess—" Ellie hesitated. Should she go see Maisie, uninvited and all? But then, why not? Maisie hadn't stood on common courtesy when she'd left Beach Cove, either.

They understood. It'd been too much to bear. Forget manners.

But even so, it'd been bewildering. Everyone had been reeling; there'd been too much loss in their small community already. And then suddenly, Maisie had been gone too. Just like that. One day she'd been there, the next she'd dropped out of sight like a cast iron anchor.

Tom made noises, but Ellie wasn't ready to let him go. There had to be more. "What sort of pizza did she order?" she demanded.

"What sort of pizza?" Tom paused. "Ma'am, I don't know if I'm allowed to give out that sort of privileged—"

"Tell me right now, Thomas."

"Oh, okay. Cheese. Plain ol' cheese pie."

"What?" Ellie frowned. "Cheese pie? No. Make the Kalamata one with rosemary and goat cheese. Use the organic rosemary."

"Mom, I can't just change her order. What if she doesn't like goat cheese?"

"Maisie wanted to get a goat so she could have goat cheese every day."

"Oh yeah? Alex never said anything about goats. Why didn't they get one?"

"Um..." Ellie tried to remember. When she did, she smiled. "She thought about it for a few days, and then she said that she already had goat cheese whenever she wanted. She just bought it at the market."

"She didn't think the store-bought cheese was any good?"

"No, she loved it."

"Right."

"She probably never told Alex about the goat, so you didn't hear about it."

"Yeah." Her son's voice went quiet. "Probably."

"So use goat cheese," Ellie said gently. "And I'll deliver it."

"Mom. You already messed with her order. Think maybe you shouldn't just show up on her doorstep?"

Ellie sighed. "Why, are you worried about your reputation? Think she'll give you a bad review online?"

"I'm worried... I don't know that I'm worried. Seems pushy though."

Ellie shrugged. "I'm not letting her leave without seeing her."

"Think she changed?"

Ellie bit the inside corner of her mouth. It'd been a decade since she'd seen her best friend. It'd been a decade since any of them had really heard from Maisie. "I expect she has," she said, and now it was her own voice that was quiet.

"Yeah."

There was a moment of silence. Then background buzzing on Tom's end, the words muffled. "Shoot, I forgot to pour out that—Mom, I got to go, we're busy."

"I'll be down in twenty for the pizza."

"I'll have it ready." Tom hung up.

Ellie pushed the phone into the back pocket of her jeans.

Maisie was back in town.

When she'd left, life had gone on in Beach Cove. But for months, it'd been like living on a ship that had lost its figurehead in a storm. They'd all drifted, aimless, waters undeclared.

The girls still met now and then. Ran across each other at the market or the post office, but it wasn't the same. They'd all agonized when Alex went missing. They'd all frozen in horror when Robert took his own life. Shocked and frightened, they'd all turned to their own families.

Everyone had tried to make their marriage work a little better. Everyone still hugged their kids a little longer, a little tighter, a lot more often.

Ellie checked the time. Ten minutes until she had to leave to pick up the pizza.

Ten minutes was plenty of time for a couple of calls. They should know what was going on. She let her finger hover over the speed dial.

Sam or Cate?

Sam could be stubborn. Cate was nice all around, poor thing. She'd be a better wrap-up, more likely to support Ellie's decision to go and see Maisie.

"Ellie?" Sam sounded as if she'd been sleeping.

"Did I wake you? Guess what. Maisie is back."

"Yep."

Yep? Sam should be dazed, not yepping the big news. Ellie narrowed her eyes. "Do you know something I don't, Samantha? I call you the minute I have information and you—"

"I know nothing." Sam blew air into Ellie's ear, making the line hum. "I just had a feeling."

"Oh for crying out loud, Sam, the woman's been gone for…since forever. Nine, ten years, and she hasn't called once." Ellie frowned. "Why aren't you surprised? I almost fell off my chair when I heard."

"I don't know." Sam cleared her throat. "Just seemed like it was time for her to come back, didn't it?"

Ellie shook her head. "What are you talking about? It didn't seem like that at all. There's no way I saw this coming."

Sam sighed. "Forget I said anything. You're right. There's no reason she should come back as far as we know."

"True." Ellie pressed her lips together. Right. Maisie would only come back if she had a reason. A reason other than her friends. "Do you think—something has changed?" Her heart hiccupped. Was there news?

"I think it must've," Sam murmured. "Yes, something must've happened. Have you talked to her? How do you know she's back? Did you see her?"

"She ordered food at the Café, to be delivered to Beach House. Tom told me. He said she didn't give her name right away."

"Oh boy, is she trying to hide?" Sam didn't sound sleepy anymore. "Ha. She's come to the wrong place for that. What exactly did she say to Tommy?"

Ellie nodded. This was more like it. "Only that she wanted a pizza delivered to her house. Cheese."

"Cheese? Hmm, strange. Is she alone?"

"I—don't know." It hadn't occurred to Ellie that Maisie could've brought someone with her. "It's possible. Could be she's married again and has kids, right?"

"Wouldn't that be so weird."

"I mean, good for her."

"Sure."

Ellie inhaled, breathing over the odd feeling curdling in her belly. "I'm going over there. I'm delivering her pizza."

Surprise thinned Sam's voice. "Really? You think that's a good idea?"

"I'm not sure I care." Ellie shrugged, aware Sam couldn't see.

"Did you say a cheese pizza?"

"I know. I told Tom to upgrade."

Sam hummed doubtfully. "What if she really wants a cheese pie? Maisie might've completely reinvented herself. She also wants to be left alone."

"I'm not giving Maisie that choice," Ellie said simply. "It's my son's restaurant, and it's goat cheese pizza. She doesn't have to eat it if she doesn't like it. And I'm delivering for the family business. Bam. Deal with it, everyone."

Sam chuckled. "Well, if that's how it is, good luck. I hope it goes well."

Ellie hesitated. "Do you want me to call when I get back?"

"No. No, that's your little adventure, Ells. If Maisie wants to get in touch with me, she's got my number."

"You're still mad. Ten years later."

Sam scoffed into the phone. "No, I'm not."

Ellie raised an eyebrow. Sam could be as stubborn as a limpet. "I'll let you know how it went."

"No, I—"

"And then we'll take it from there. We don't know how we feel yet."

"We do!"

"No," Ellie repeated firmly. "We don't. We never heard her side of the story."

"Whatever."

Ellie smiled. When Sam was grumpy like that, she was just protecting her feelings. "It's okay to feel hurt, Samantha, but we don't let that stand in the way of communication and connection," Ellie said primly.

"Stop it."

"And I love *you*. So, I'll let you know," Ellie said. "And then we'll see."

"You do what you want."

"Yes," Ellie confirmed. "Sam? One last thing..."

Order Beach Cove Home to keep reading!

About the Author

Nellie Brooks writes heartwarming women's fiction with relatable characters who face challenges ranging from bitter to sweet. After years of traveling the world, she turned to writing fiction. Her books are set in Maine, where Nellie likes to spend time on the beach with her family. Visit www.nelliebrooks.com to subscribe to her newsletter and get a free novella. You can also follow Nellie on Facebook and BookBub.

Made in the USA
Monee, IL
14 March 2023